VICTORIAN SLUM GIRL'S DREAM

A HISTORICAL VICTORIAN SAGA

DOLLY PRICE

PUREREAD.COM

CONTENTS

CHAPTER ONE

1851

Penny didn't remember her father, but she sobbed at his funeral just the same, as much as Mamma did. Her father had gone away after she was born. He'd had to go into the Queen's Service. Grandma was not crying. She looked grim, as she looked when the landlord was banging on the door and she was pretending they were all out. Penny sat in the pew and stared at the plain wood coffin. It was very hard to believe that her father, the man she did not remember, was in that long box. She did not like the thought and picked up the corner of her mother's black shawl and held it up to her eyes so that she would not have to look at it.

"I'm glad that's over," her mother said later on, poking the fire after the neighbours had gone home. "But now I have to get used to being without him."

"Emma, Harry hasn't been here for years."

"But I'll miss the thought of him coming back, Mother."

Grandma snorted. She slammed the teapot on the table. The action spoke loudly. Penny was surprised.

"Why didn't Papa leave the Castle sometimes to come and see us, Mamma?" asked Penny, looking up from her rag doll, Nancy. She'd been plaiting her hair.

"He couldn't, Penny. The Queen required 'im to stay." Her mother answered.

"It's not Royalty as abides in Lancaster Castle," muttered Grandma darkly. "The tea's ready, come to the table, Emma."

"And he would have been able to leave next November, and come 'ome." Mrs. Fowler lamented.

"When 'is sentence was up," muttered Grandma Pyke, pouring.

"Why wouldn't the Queen let him come home to see us?" Penny asked.

"Seven years for river piracy," continued Grandma Pyke, spooning sugar in.

"It was just a bag of coal, Mother! For the child!"

"He shouldn't a done it! Drink yer tea." She pushed the teacup toward Emma.

Penny did not understand. She frowned and unplaited Nancy's hair again, shaking it out, while her mother and grandmother drank their tea.

"Come an 'ave some milk, Penny." Her mother said then.

"If Papa was in the Queen's Service," she said, "The Queen would 'ave paid 'im a lot of money, wouldn't she? If Papa is dead, can we 'ave it now? Maybe we can get a new house where we can live in the upstairs as well as the downstairs!"

"It's time to tell her," said her grandmother, eating a biscuit a neighbour had brought.

"No. We moved from Battle Row so she'd never have to put up with teasing and taunting, and why tell her now?"

"Tell me what?"

"Your Papa was in prison, Penny," said her grandmother. "He was put in prison for stealing coal comin' from Worsley. Seven years 'ard labour."

Her mother slammed her cup upon her saucer. "Why did you tell her, Mother? Why? I didna want 'her to know! She didn't have to know! Ever!"

Penny put down her doll.

"I thought he was in Lancaster Castle!" she wailed, more angry than upset.

"Lancaster Castle is a prison." Said her grandmother, grimly.

"Mamma, if Papa was in prison, he was a bad man!"

"Your father was not a bad man!" said her mother doggedly.

"He was a thief," said Mrs. Pyke. "He was no good."

Penny put her doll down abruptly.

"You told me, Mamma, that Papa would come out of the Queens Service and we wouldn't be poor anymore!!" she cried. "I thought we were going to live in a proper house, like the Eglintons!"

She burst into loud, angry tears and threw herself on the mat, weeping.

"See what you've done, Mother!" cried Emma. "She's not mourning her own father anymore, because you changed her mind about 'im! She used to love 'im, now look there, she don't!"

"Oh don't be a ninny, Emma. She would 'ave found out sooner than later."

"And you should never 'ave taken her to the Eglinton's! It's made her down in the mouth. She's always going on about us being poor now! Get up off the floor, Penelope Fowler. Stop goin' on like that. I don't like it!"

Penny ignored her. Her mother continued to admonish her for her tantrum, but it did not cease for twenty minutes.

"You always give 'er her own way, that's why she won't listen to me!" cried Mrs. Fowler to her mother.

"And what would you 'ave done without me for the last seven years?" retorted the older woman.

Later that evening, Mrs. Fowler scolded her daughter in her tiny room which was little more than a closet, as to why it was wrong to throw strops like she had. It was all right for a small child, but she was too old to throw herself on the mat and scream. It wouldn't do.

Penny felt genuinely sorry. "I won't do it again, Mamma."

"You'll 'ave to learn to control yourself, child. You're old enough now. Life isn't easy and you won't gert your own way in it. And – your father loved you, it was for you 'e stole the coal, it was the dead of winter and you cryin' with the cold. He was desperate, 'e was. Tell me you still love your father, after what 'e tried to do for you, and was spendin' seven long years breakin' stones for it and died afore 'e could come home."

Penny immediately felt guilty, and yet she did not feel it was fair that she should feel guilty. But her heart softened.

"I did so want to be rich, Mamma. I thought we would be, after the Queen paid Papa."

"I never said we'd be rich, Penny. We will never be rich. Not us. Put that out of your 'ead."

Penny slid down in the bed, glum and unhappy. She said nothing. Her mother kissed her forehead, took the candle and went to the kitchen.

"I'm sorry I told 'er about her father," muttered Mrs. Pyke. "You're the parent, and I had no right to interfere. You're in mourning now, that I know, and I should've been better to you today, and Harry not cold."

"Oh never mind, Mother, what's done is done. I don't know what I would 'ave done without you all these years. And of course you 'ave to bring her to the Eglintons when I'm at the Mill. You can't leave her 'ere on her own. Let's 'ave another brew, it's been a long day, and I'm that tired, I could lie down and sleep for three days. Poor Harry, I was so lookin' forward to 'im comin' home soon. And for 'im to meet our Penny, and how she took after 'im, with her light hair, but more yellow, and eyes so blue like his." She took up the framed daguerreotype from the mantelpiece and kissed the man in his Sunday best, on their wedding day eight years before. He'd been a bargeman by trade, not regular work, and the night he stole the coal had been freezing cold. She'd been at home in their room on Battle Street. He'd never come home that night and the following day she'd got a message to say he'd been arrested. After his sentencing she'd gone to live with her mother, and then they'd moved to the Red Bank area near the railway lines. Emma had found work in Packer's Mill where she worked long days sitting at a loom. She had a limp since childhood, and could not join her mother in her laundry business, as much of it entailed standing and walking long distances.

Penny helped her Grandma while she washed linen for a few of the rich houses in Clifton Walk. For some time now, she had been walking to the Eglintons with her, collecting their soiled linen, taking it home and returning it washed, dried and ironed. Mrs. Eglinton thought her laundress lived in a good cottage with her own well and lines and hedges to dry sheets, but she obtained her water from a pump, and artfully paid her friend Mrs. Browne to dry the sheets in the back garden behind her cottage. Mrs. Eglinton, she thought, would not like her linen going to this area near the railway line, a poor area known for its bad sanitation and smoky air. People were so fussy now about things like cleanliness and open air.

CHAPTER TWO

"Are you ready, Penny?" Mrs. Pyke took the hamper of clean, ironed linen from the table and settled it on her hip. Penny carried a small packet consisting of their lunch, a jam sandwich. They left the flat, locking the door behind them. It was a dry day. Even on rainy days they walked most of the way to Eglinton's, with sheets of oilskin covering the dry linens under the lid.

The street was busy this Friday morning. On their way, Grandma stopped to speak to Mrs. Sully, who told her that her daughter's baby had died that morning. This was not unusual, every other day Grandma was stopped on the street to be told somebody had died, and very often it was a child. Penny pondered it as they made their way to the railway line. They would follow the sidings for a short distance.

"Why do children die, Grandma?" she asked while she hopped from sleeper to sleeper. Grandma always let her do that on this straight stretch on the way to Eglinton's.

"Why they sicken, don't they, and die."

"People who are young aren't supposed to die."

"You think too much for a girl your age. Babies get fevers and they're too weak to fight 'em."

"I won't die, will I? Until I'm old?"

The familiar rumble emerged from the town end of the track behind them.

"You'll die in a minute if you don't 'op off that track now. If your mother knew I was letting you do that, she'd be angry wiv me."

"Oh I won't tell her, Grandma." Penny jumped to the side and Grandma grasped her arm firmly and drew her to her side. They stopped to watch the approaching engine. The driver hooted a warning and Penny waved, and he waved back. Grandma coughed, muttering about how bad Manchester had got with trains screeching, and they made folks restless to go places when they should be content to stay at home. To Mrs. Pyke, great evil was to be found in this new fad.

They reached one of Manchester's many arches soon after, with Grandma uttering her usual opinion that the city was forever ruined, and left the railway, entering a lane that brought them to Berrybush Road, and walked along that for a bit before turning into Clifton Walk. An area popular with the successful shipping and textile merchants and their associated professions, it was a wide, new street with young trees planted along the pathways. Each gracious house sat in its own park at the end of a long avenue. Some of the homes were of a modern style; others had been built to mimic Italian or Gothic architecture. The Eglinton residence, with *'Eglinton House'* in fancy letters worked into the wrought-iron design of the high black gate, was red brick with bay windows and looked far less ostentatious than many of its neighbours.

They walked up the avenue. Penny looked up at the house as it loomed higher and higher. The recent disappointment enveloped her again. She would never live in a house like this. She felt resentful; cheated.

"Can't we go in the front door, Grandma?" she asked, looking longingly at the several stone steps flanked by short pillars with chubby stone cherubs keeping watch. The door itself was bright red and the top part was stained glass. How she'd love to go in the front door! What was behind it? She longed to know.

"Gracious no, child. What's come over you?" They walked around to the back, the gravel crunching underfoot.

Sarah, a maid, was in the kitchen. She went to find Mrs. Eglinton.

"Mrs. Pyke, good to see you – but I was expecting you yesterday, you know!" said the Lady of the house when she came down.

The truth was that Mrs. Browne had not had the linen dry, due to her baking a cake for a spoiled, lazy son who came and went as he pleased, but Mrs. Pyke had her answer ready.

"Did it not rain here on Tuesday?" she asked, feigning surprise.

"Not a drop, Mrs. Pyke."

"We had heavy showers, I had to take in the sheets twice – sodden they were, each time, in and out I was to the clothesline, all day long, it was a waste of a day, I can tell you."

"At least we have them now." Mrs. Eglinton said, suppressing a smile.

Penny had not taken her eyes from her, and at last Mrs. Eglinton saw her and said: "Sarah, get Penny a biscuit."

With the biscuit in her hand, Penny wandered outside while Mrs. Eglinton and Grandma checked the linen against the book. She often went off on her own. There was a dog called Patch who bounded over to her, and a cat who ran off. After petting Patch, she walked into the kitchen garden and out the other side, around a path lined with tall bushes and found her way to the front garden. As she emerged from the path, something hit her hard on her shoulder. A ball dropped to the ground.

"Oh I say, I'm very sorry," said the Eglinton son, who was some years older than she. "I didn't know there was anybody there. Are you hurt?"

"No, not at all," Penny said.

"Have you come with your grandmother?"

"Yes, she's in the kitchen." Penny's eyes wandered to the house. "You live in a lovely house," she said.

"It's all right, isn't it?"

"I wish I lived in a house like that." She rubbed her upper arm absently where the ball had hit it.

"I did hurt you, didn't I?"

"No, well only a bit."

Martin seemed uncomfortable for a moment.

"I say, would you like to see inside the house?" he asked brightly.

"Could I?"

"Yes, of course you could. Come on."

He dropped the cricket bat and went toward the front door. Penny followed. The front door!

CHAPTER THREE

U p the stone steps, past the chubby angels, and Master Eglinton pushed the door open in front of him as Penny followed. She was in a hallway. There was a shining table by the wall and soft rugs underfoot.

Master Eglinton pushed open a door on the left.

"Here's the drawing room."

It was like a picture in a fairytale book. Long blue curtains. White wallpaper with little red roses. Paintings on the walls. A large white fireplace, and a big mirror over it with a golden frame. Enormous chairs that looked like they belonged in Buckingham Palace. A couch with white cushions, and little white tables here and there. A carpet under her feet, grey with small red roses and green leaves. She felt she had stepped into Heaven. She touched one of the tables, looking gingerly at Master Eglinton in case he disapproved.

"It's marble, do you like it?" he asked, smiling.

"Marble," repeated Penny. "Yes, I do like it."

He sprang to a far wall and threw open the double doors, revealing another room with a long table and chairs. A vase of bright flowers adorned the table. The same wallpaper and carpet and curtains met her. A cabinet by the wall held a set of silver on top, teapots, urns, and bowls. Another big mirror with a gold frame. Everything shone.

He ran past her and into the hallway again, bounded up the stairs, and she followed.

"My mother's room," he threw open another door down a hallway. She entered behind him.

The largest bed she had ever seen, the four posts hung with patterned curtains. Large white pillows edged in lace. The floral bedspread looked inviting, she touched it, wondering what Master Eglinton would say, but again he did not say anything, so she drew her hand across it. She caught sight of the dressing table, with fans, perfumes, hairbrushes, combs and a hand mirror and all the things a Lady should have.

"Come on, see my room now."

She did not like his room so much, with its maps on the walls and boy's things strewn about, but his sister Matilda's room enchanted her. It was like a princess' room. So soft and white and lacy. A chest of drawers had three dolls sitting on top, three real china dolls, dressed in pretty clothes with hats to match. Artwork adorned the walls, drawings of Eglinton House, and of vases of flowers.

"Can I sit on the bed?" she asked. He nodded.

So soft! The sheets felt smooth and silky under her fingertips. Penny thought of her own small cot-bed, hard with rough sheets.

"Can I see inside the wardrobe?" she asked.

"Of course." Master Eglinton opened the door wide. Penny saw an array of the most sumptuous clothes she had ever laid eyes upon. Dresses of every colour, in plaid and flowery patterns, each adorned with frills and ribbons and lace. Again, she put out her hand to touch them, to make sure they were real. The upper shelf was covered in bonnets and hats and neatly folded shawls. For one girl to own all of those gowns spelled riches beyond imagining! She only had two, her blue serge and green wool, and her Sunday Best, a grey cotton with a red sash.

There was a row of books on a wall shelf.

"What are those books?" she asked.

"*Andersen's Fairy Tales* and *Edgeworth's Stories for Children*." Master Eglinton began. "And poetry."

"So Matilda can read?"

"Oh yes, of course she can. She even writes poetry. And all the drawings on the walls are her work."

"What age is Matilda?"

"She's twelve."

"Do you want to see anything else?" he asked, after they had emerged. "There's Father's study – yes – let's go there." He darted across the landing and they entered a large room with a desk. Bookcases ran along three walls.

"So many books!"

"Can you read?" the young Master asked.

She shook her head.

"Aren't you going to go to school?" he asked then.

"I don't know."

"Matilda goes to school. I do too, I came home yesterday for the Easter holidays. Matilda will be here tomorrow."

"Do you like Father's globe?" he asked with enthusiasm, spinning it slowly. "Look, there's Peru. That's where Father is at the moment."

"Peru?" she looked. She'd never seen a map before and her puzzlement showed.

"It's a country in South America." He said kindly.

She nodded. She'd heard of America.

"Where's England?" she asked.

He showed her England, Ireland, and France.

"And there's the Arctic, which has snow and ice all the year around. Nobody can live there except the Eskimos. And here's the Equator, which is hot all the time. And England is sort of in the middle of the two, which means we're a mixture of heat and cold."

"Why is your father in Peru?" she asked him.

"He has business there. He has an import business and ships. He brings cotton out, and brings back fruits that don't grow in England."

As they returned downstairs after viewing some extra bedrooms, unused but ready for guests, Penny was silent. She lingered behind Master Eglinton and ran her hand along the wallpaper – it was soft as silk.

"I'd love to live in a house like this." she blurted.

Master Eglinton, who's Christian name was Martin, turned around. He saw the shabbily-dressed girl in her drab shawl and bonnet and wondered if perhaps he should not have shown her the house. He thought it would be a treat for her, after hitting her with the ball. And she was so sporting about being hit too. But she seemed to have taken the tour as a revelation in what she did not have. He hoped he had not made her unhappy. She was looking at him with a question in her eyes.

"You have to be – educated," he said awkwardly. Because he did not want to say, *Your parents have to have enough money.*

"You have to learn to read to live in a house like this," He went on, in a tone that was a little insistent, but he felt very uncomfortable, and felt he had to give some advice and that was all he could think of. "I had better take you back to the garden. Your grandmother may be looking for you."

Grandmamma was cross with her for running off. She was astounded that Master Eglinton had shown Penny his house, the main rooms, even the bedrooms. But then she was envious and wanted to know every detail while they sat on a bench and ate their sandwich. Did she see any Chinese vases? Tell her again about the silver in the dining-room. What colour was Mrs. Eglinton's bedchamber? Were her bedcurtains velvet, very soft to touch? How big was the mirror over her dressing-table? On the walk home, Penny hardly said a word, except that she wanted to be 'educated.' Grandma made no reply, and Penny was dissatisfied.

CHAPTER FOUR

Penny doggedly persisted in her quest for education. Her mother said they could not afford to pay, and that if she was to go to school, it was to be the Ragged School. Her grandmother opposed the entire idea.

"What are you educatin' 'er for, might I ask? She can learn reading and arithmetic from me, enough as to how to keep a book for the laundry. I have enough learnin' to run my laundry, don't I?"

"I want to be able to read books," said Penelope, thinking of those she had seen in Matilda's room. It was not so much that she wanted to know what was between the covers as that it was a step to her dream of becoming wealthy. Master Eglinton had said so.

"How can I do without 'er, she helps in all sorts of ways," said Mrs. Pyke crossly. "She can stir the coppers out back, young as she is. She helps me pull the wet sheets out. She helps me fold the sheets too."

"She can still help you with all that," said Emma patiently. "She needn't go to school on Mondays, and the folding can be done after school on Wednesdays. She doesn't need to be 'ere when the washing is dryin' over at Mrs. Browne's, does she? And she can't iron yet neither."

"I need 'er to come with me on Thursdays," sulked her Grandma. "I don't want to walk all that way on my own. She's company."

"She can go with you on Thursdays, as she always has. She'll still 'ave three days in school."

So it was settled. Penny would go to school three days a week for four hours each day. She was exultant.

CHAPTER FIVE

Penny applied herself well and learned easily. The books were shared between the children. She wanted books of her own, but that was not possible.

On Mondays, she helped with the Wash, and on Thursdays or an occasional Friday if the drying had been delayed by rain, she went to Clifton Walk. Every time she entered the Eglinton driveway, she looked up at the house and it made her more determined than ever to become rich. She met Miss Matilda Eglinton a few times when she accompanied her grandmother to the kitchen to receive the laundry. She was in awe of her. Her hair was in perfect ringlets around her shoulders, her dress had three flounces in the skirt and little red ribbons set in lace on the bodice. She decided to study even harder.

Within a year, she could read and write well, and add, subtract and multiply. She rarely spoke of her progress at home. She was afraid that if her mother and Grandma knew how good she was, that they would take her out, thinking she'd had enough. The teachers never met the parents, so she was safe. The second year began without any protest from either Grandma or her mother. But the third year, when she was nine, her grandmother became ill and Penny was afraid that she would have to leave school to look after her and do more, both laundry and housework. Grandma had rheumatics. She could no longer work as she used to, nor walk well. Clifton Walk was now quite beyond her. Penny had to take over the household work and the Wash, while Grandma still managed the ironing.

Penny was too small to manage Washday all by herself, so she enlisted the help of Sam, a strong but simple boy who lived next door to pull the wet sheets out of the copper and into the wringer. Grandma gave him two pennies for this. On Thursdays, her mother asked Sam to walk with Penny to Clifton Walk, for his lunch of a jam sandwich. It was worth it to him, and his mother was very pleased to see him do something useful. Sam waited for her outside while she went alone into the Eglinton's house.

One day, she met Master Eglinton who was going out of the gate with a tall, spindly gentleman in frock coat and beaver hat – a surly look about him, she thought. Sarah had told her that Mr. Eglinton was expected home from a long voyage, and she supposed this must be him. Except for his dark hair and high forehead he did not resemble the young Master. He had a dark beard, a severe appearance and a scowl. She didn't take to him.

Master Eglinton nodded silently to her, and Penny nodded back. She wondered how long his father would stay before he left again. She wanted to ask him if she could borrow a book or two from Matilda. She wanted to keep reading, and was determined not to forget anything she'd learned.

After two months, she was pleased to learn that Mr. Eglinton had left on another voyage. She hoped to see Master Eglinton soon, thankfully it was holiday time, and he was in the front lawn practicing cricket. He often took no notice of her, as their paths did not cross, but this time, she stood on the path until he saw her standing staring at him. He came over.

"Is there something you need, Penny?" he asked, in some bewilderment.

"I have a favour to ask you, Master Eglinton." She began, a little nervously, but boldly too, for she was determined.

"I had to leave school -" she said.

"Oh hard luck!"

"- so my education is not complete yet. But I want to keep readin'. But –" she swallowed. It was hard to admit what she had to say. "I've no books worth readin'. I was going to ask you if you could lend me a book or two of Miss Eglinton's."

He did not know what to say to this. He didn't think Matilda would approve of her books being lent to the laundress. He could, of course, lend her his own books, but he wasn't sure that it was a good idea. He did not want to hurt her feelings, but normally, one did not lend things to servants.

"I say, I know what would be much better," he said in an inspiration. "You simply must join the library."

"The library!"

"Yes, there's a library that lends out books. You must get a borrower's card, and you can take out two books for a few weeks, and then return them when you've finished."

"Where can I find the library?"

"It's in Campfield." He threw the ball in the air, and caught it.

"Where is Campfield?"

"It's – not very far, I'm sure from anywhere in Manchester." He seemed to want to get back to his practice, and stepped back.

Penny walked slowly to the back door. It niggled her that the young Master had not wanted to lend her books, either his or his sister's. Nobody wanted to really know people like her. She saw that. And how he stepped back, as if there was almost something wrong with her wanting to improve her mind now, when he had recommended it.

Still, the library idea was very appealing. How could she find out where the library was?

CHAPTER SIX

I t was Tuesday, and after sweeping the floors and cleaning the house, Penny set out for the Ragged School. She would ask the schoolmaster about the library. If anybody knew, he would.

"You're the first child who has ever asked about joining the Library," Mr. Digby said, astonished. "It's new, and very popular. Boys! Boys!" he called to some bigger lads who were racing from the classroom as if released from a prison. "Now here's a girl who wants to join the library, *a girl*! Doesn't that make you ashamed of yourselves, boys?" he shouted after them.

The boys ran off.

"I do not know about girls joining the library," he said doubtfully. "There's a Boys Reading Room, but there isn't any for girls. What put it into your head?"

"I want to improve my mind." she insisted.

"You want to teach? Here in the Ragged School perhaps?"

Penny felt angry. She did not want to teach in the Ragged School! She wanted to be above, far above that!

Mr. Digby patted her on the head and walked away. She turned away slowly, disappointed.

"Penny!" called a teacher, Miss Villiers. "I heard you say you wished to join the Library. I think it is an excellent idea."

Miss Villiers was a missionary from a good family, who devoted her free time to teaching poor children.

"I cannot take you to the library," she said, "But I do have a borrower's card, and I shall take out one book for you a month. But you must be very careful with it, for they expect their books to be returned in very good condition. Keep it away from small children and dogs and cats and fire and water, and don't turn down the corners, don't write on it or make any marks."

Penny beamed. She promised to guard the books and thanked her.

CHAPTER SEVEN

1856

"Your father is coming home, children." announced Mrs. Eglinton one day, with as much enthusiasm as she could muster. "He will be here in six weeks. He writes that he hopes to see marked improvement in you both, and especially in you, Martin."

The children became anxious. Eglinton House felt oppressive when their father was at home. He treated his home as a sort of visiting port, only staying as long as he had to, before going away again. His visits generally lasted ten days to begin with, and then he left for Bristol, or Liverpool, or Leeds, where he had business. He never liked to spend more than ten days with his wife and children.

Mrs. Eglinton accepted the situation. In truth, she and her husband had little in common. She had a sweet, affectionate nature, and it was entirely lost on this cold-hearted man. She'd married him at the behest of her father, a business partner. She looked upon his visits home as a necessary evil.

He returned to make himself feared rather than loved, she thought.

She wondered what he would say to the redecorated dining room. It had cost forty pounds and was a quiet dusky pink and grey. And she had bought a piano as well, she felt almost ill at having to defend it. But all of her friends and neighbours had a piano. And when they visited, they played for her. She enjoyed that. She was lonely with the children away at school.

She would have to tell Dr Aldridge to keep out of sight. The brother of one of her friends, he accompanied his sister Anne on evening visits when the children were away at school. It was entirely innocent, but Mr. Eglinton might not think so.

The day came, and the carriage rolled up to the door. He alighted and surveyed his property with a critical rather than a fond eye. His wife and children came down the steps to meet him. He embraced them, told Martin he expected him to be taller, and Matilda that she was too tall. For his wife, there was a hope expressed that she had not overspent on the house while he'd been away.

He'd brought gifts for them, Peruvian shawls for his wife and daughter, and a curved Chilean knife for his son, which Martin was very pleased with. He ate dinner, commenting that the silver need not have been gotten out for him, and he hoped they were not using it every evening. Mrs. Eglinton assured him that they were not, but it was a special occasion, was it not? He went to his study soon after to look about there.

He came downstairs later to the drawing room.

"You redecorated, Mary, didn't you? And what is that – a pianoforte? Nobody plays in this house. I hope Matilda isn't taking lessons. She draws and paints, that's enough. I have no time for women overloading themselves with accomplishments, all to get a husband. I'll get a husband for you, when the time comes," he added generously to his daughter.

"Thank you, sir." Matilda resolved immediately to get her own husband.

"Don't get too tall."

"I will do my best, sir." Matilda blushed and looked down. She was self-conscious about her height.

He walked about, poured himself a whiskey, and drank it.

"How is your Latin, Martin?"

"Coming on well, sir."

"*Caesars Gallic Wars*."

Martin began to recite the first chapter, but his father put his hand up after a paragraph.

"And your Spanish?"

"Spanish, Father? We don't do Spanish now, at Grevilles."

"What's this? I sent you there with the particular intention of learning Spanish!"

"The Spanish Master left, and he was not replaced."

"Why was I not informed of this?" Mr. Eglinton glared at his wife.

"I did write," she said. "And I said I would await your instruction."

He poured himself another whiskey.

His wife was about to object to his imbibing, but thought better of it. Let him drink himself to sleep, and she would not complain! He could sleep in his dressing room. She dreaded his homecomings. She'd had no more children, because many years ago she had had to take mercury for a disease he had brought home with him. It had made her sterile, but she had lived. The children, of course, knew nothing about that.

"Father, are you quite well?" Martin asked suddenly.

"I am well. Why do you ask?"

"The voyage was a long one -" Martin did not want to say that he noticed a tremble in his hand, a high colour in his face.

The tea was brought in, and Matilda poured.

"Indian tea," said her father, appearing to be happy for the first time since he had come in. "None of you ask me what it is we drink on board."

"Besides whiskey, Father?" asked Matilda, with a little bold humour.

"What do you drink on board ship, dear?" asked Mrs. Eglinton.

"China tea. We pick it up in Hong Kong, along with the passengers."

"I did not know you took passengers, Father." Martin said.

"We do. All the way to Peru, sometimes."

"Why would Chinese people want to go to Peru?" he asked. "It seems like a long way."

"For work, of course. Mary, I do think you've spent too much money on this room. It does not look well. Why such a large mirror over the fireplace? What did that cost?"

"That was a gift from Miss Aldridge on my fortieth birthday."

"You turned forty? I declare I never knew. When was that?"

CHAPTER EIGHT

P enny came in the front gate and made her way to the back door as usual, and entered the kitchen. Sarah was Cook now and she was baking there.

"Oh, the Lord of the Manor is back," said Sarah. "There's a completely different air in the house when he's here. I do pity the children. He's always bellowing. His poor wife –" she ceased talking as they heard footsteps.

"Good morning, Penny."

"Good morning, Mrs. Eglinton."

"You do not mind coming by yourself, along by the railway?"

"No, Mrs. Eglinton. Since Sam, my neighbour died, I found a girl whose mother washes for the people in Grant Road, so we arrange to walk together, the same day. Then I only have to walk a little way by myself."

"What did your father do, Penny?"

"He was Captain of a barge, Mrs. Eglinton." Penny did not mind stretching the truth.

"And he died when you were little?"

"Very little, Mrs. Eglinton. I hardly remember him at all."

"How sad. Your mother works, does she?"

"Yes, in the Mill. She's a supervisor over fifty girls." Another stretch.

"Why did you not go into the Mill too, Penny? Are you interested in doing some other kind of work?"

"This, Mrs. Eglinton." She patted her hamper.

"Always? I would think there's no possibility for advancement. Do you mind if I ask you what age you are now?"

"I'm twelve, Mrs. Eglinton."

"Twelve! You look older than that. I thought you were getting on to fourteen. You're too young to go into service, then. But when you're fourteen, there will be a situation for you here if you want it. We'll fit you into the kitchen or the parlour, or wherever the need is. Goodness you seem much older than twelve!"

"How so, Mrs. Eglinton? I'm not big."

"Oh, your height hasn't anything to do with it. It's in your demeanour."

"*Demeen - your?*"

"Yes, the way you carry yourself in the world. We had better count the linen, hadn't we?"

Penny went away deep in thought. *'The way you carry yourself in the world'.* She liked the sound of that. It made her feel older, and wiser, and all the things she hoped people thought she was. Mrs. Eglinton made it sound like an advantage.

She had read many books by now. Miss Villiers was faithful in delivering a book every month to her. Many of the books were about rich people. Gentlefolk. And only educated people, she thought, read them too, because they were very hard to read.

At the beginning, she'd been unhappy because of all the big words that she did not understand. Her mother and Grandma did not know what they meant either, and were inclined to laugh at her for persisting with books. Not understanding what she was reading had almost made her give up, and she had told Miss Villiers about it. The teacher had said:

"You need a dictionary, Penny!"

"What's a dick-shun-ary, Miss?"

"A book of words. My father has several – I shall ask him for one for you."

And so she presented her with a dictionary, a book full of words and their explanations, and showed her how to use it. Penny was delighted with the gift. She kept it with her every time she read a book, and was able to look up words she did not know, and if she did not know the words used to define the word, she looked them up in turn.

Her mother and grandmother thought she was daft.

"I want to be rich," she defended herself. "I will be rich, you'll see! And when I'm rich, we can leave this horrid place and live in a large house with servants."

"Education isn't going to make you rich," said her mother. "You 'ave to know people! To get *patronage*, that is."

"Where did you get that word, Emma? *Patronage!*" Grandma laughed.

"I know it, because Mrs. Grange at the Mill has a cousin who has a friend who's an artist, if you don't mind, and 'e has the *patronage* of Sir William Sherrill. But for all that, 'e's still poor! Lives in a freezing attic wiv his paintings!"

They laughed together. But Penny was worried. It was not enough to be educated, then? She looked up *patronage,* unwilling to admit to her mother that she did not know it.

Patronage – the support given to a patron.

Patron – a person who provides economic or other support to another.

"Penny, you can always marry Money," said Grandma jokingly.

"Don't, Mother. Don't put that into her 'ead. I have no time at all for women who marry for money, and not love."

"Love! Where did *Love* get you, I ask?"

This was a sensitive subject, Penny knew, so she changed it by asking if they'd like tea.

Marry money. She could, she supposed, keep it in mind, but at twelve, she was far too young to think about marriage!

"I want you to forgit what Grandma said today," her mother said when she entered her little room to bid her goodnight. "About marrying money. She was just joking. I know you want to do well for yourself, and better'n me. But if you think that you can buy 'appiness tha' way, you're wrong. When you're seventeen or so, I 'ope you marry a good tradesman, sober and reliable. You shouldn't want to go 'igher, or you'll be disappointed. There's many a poor girl that got a rich admirer, who ended up ruining 'er life, ending all her 'opes and dreams o' becoming a Lady."

"Have no fears, Mamma. A rich man would be very foolish to marry a poor girl."

"How do you think so much about these matters?"

"In a book I read, a young gentleman married a penniless girl and tired of her and drowned her."

"What a silly story!"

"It was a true story, Mamma!"

"You read too much, girl. It mithers me to see you know so much that your own mother and grandmother don't know! I'm not sure readin' is good for you, and I don't know what you're readin'. Nobody else around here reads, not the Matthews, not the Masons or the Brooks or the Cartwrights. People remark on you readin', as if it was an oddity. And then there's the cost of candles. We're burning too many. Give up those books!"

"I don't care what anybody thinks, Mamma. They're ignorant people."

"What a 'orrible thing to say of our neighbours! Mrs. Matthews would give you the shirt off her back. Those books are changin' you. I 'ave a good mind to take that big dick-shun-ary of yours and start the fire with it someday."

"If you do that, Mamma, I'll never forgive you. And as for candles, I'm workin', and it's only fair I should 'ave my own candle. Don't touch my dictionary, Mamma, and don't make me give up readin', cos I'll run away if you do."

Emma knew her daughter meant what she said. She felt truly put in her place, and it wasn't right that a child of twelve should do that to her mother. None of the neighbour's girls were like her daughter. They liked to talk and gossip and play, and none of them, not one, was interested in 'improving her mind' as Penny put it. Penny had ideas above her station, and Mrs. Fowler had uneasy feelings about it.

Her own mother, though, did not see it that way.

"Wait till you see, Emma, when Penny's sixteen or seventeen, she'll fall in love with one of the Cartwright boys, a 'andsome family, or the Masons, good cobblers - and there's nothing like falling in love to make girls forget all their own plans. She'll want nothing else except to marry 'im. Don't mither yourself."

"Not my Penelope," said Emma, her lips tight. "No, you're wrong there, Mother, not 'er. She won't do owt that doesn't benefit 'erself in some way. She wants to be rich, an' I'm reet afeard for her, I am."

CHAPTER NINE

1858

"Are you ready, Martin? Stop clinging to him, Mary!"

"Two years is such a long time to be away!" cried his mother, her handkerchief at her eyes. "Why does it have to be so long?"

"Because the voyage is long and he's a grown man now."

"I have to go, Mother, let go of me. There." Martin extracted himself from his mother's loving arms and got into the carriage.

"Please write often!" wept Matilda, waving her handkerchief. "We'll miss you!"

"Women!" sighed his father as the carriage clattered down the driveway. "I get heartily sick of being around them for too long."

Martin was very pleased to go with his father to Peru. As heir to the business, he had to know every detail of Eglinton

Imports. He had finished school. He was adept at Spanish, Geography, History, Geometry, Algebra and other subjects.

They boarded the *Pride of Eglinton* a few weeks later at Liverpool, and sailed for Lisbon, where they took on more supplies for the long voyage around Cape Horn. The ship was packed with cotton from Manchester for delivery at various ports along the way.

Martin enjoyed his adventure. It was his first time outside England, and it was enthralling to see what life was like in other places, to taste the different foods, to drink the local wines or ales, to see the dark-skinned girls dressed in brilliant colours, and flashing smiles at him, instead of the demure ones he was used to at home. But he suspected that his father was rather too free with those girls.

The weather was sunny, the seas calm as they sailed south. He shared a cabin with the second mate, who was an entertaining fellow. The Captain was an old seafarer who could not bear to be on land for any length of time. Everybody was polite to Martin; as the son of one of the owners, he was given every deference and allowances were made for his youth when he gaffed.

He and his father were getting on quite well when they were at sea and Martin could not but wonder if it was the all-male atmosphere that fostered it. He saw his father's cheerful side. He thought he drank rather too much, but said little about that.

"It's good to have you along, Martin," his father said suddenly one evening as they drank a whiskey on deck. "You're quite a smart lad, and the crew all like you."

As they made their way south, the weather changed, and by the time they sailed Cape Horn, that stretch where the Atlantic and Pacific clash with inevitable tossing and roiling,

Martin was used to the pitch and roll. The night they crossed was memorable for its storm. Many ships had been lost at the Cape and he was rather relieved to round it and meet calmer seas again as they coursed towards Lima. They disembarked and lodged at La Casa Inglesa in the middle of town. His balcony looked out onto the street and he watched Lima's fashionable people go by. Watching the ladies, he was sure the voluminous veils covered faces that were beautiful.

But his father was anxious to get on with his work, and after only two days on land, they boarded a small ship to take them to the Isla de Plata, an island located only a little distance from the coastline. Martin set off with deep interest, for it was in these islands that the Eglinton fortune was made.

As they neared the small islands, a disagreeable odour came upon them on the air, overpowering the fresh breeze.

"That's the smell of the gold," said his father with glee. "I told you that our business is not fruit, didn't I? I wager you are curious as to what it is!"

"It is about time you told me, Father. But you wished to keep me in suspense! Whatever it is, it smells very bad indeed, and I'm growing more suspicious by the hour."

"The Eglinton wealth comes from bird droppings. *Guano*. Don't tell your mother; her fine friends would laugh at her and all of us."

"Bird droppings, Father?" Martin was repelled.

"Yes, bird droppings. There are high cliffs of hardened seabird droppings, and they sell for a fortune at home as fertiliser."

Martin could see the silvery outlines of the cliffs. The silver, he supposed, was the precious guano. He was dumbfounded.

Besides the Eglinton party, there was only a Captain, a First Mate and three hands on this ship. But there were other ships bearing upon the islands for the purpose of collecting the fertiliser. There was no proper port on the islands, so they moored a little way offshore, and a rowing boat was made ready.

"You understand, Martin, that none of what you are about to see is to be reported at home." instructed his father with gravity as they were rowed in, causing Martin to raise an eyebrow.

Nearing the cliffs, Martin could see, dotted in several places upon their faces, small armies of men swinging pickaxes. The mined matter fell to the ground below, where they were gathered by other teams and borne to waiting boats.

The smell was almost unbearable; he felt sick, and gagged.

"You'll get used to it." remarked his father.

They were met on the shore by a man with a weather beaten face who greeted them profusely. He was introduced as Mr. Hammond.

"I'm expecting more cargo; I'm losing about twenty a week," he said, jerking his head toward the cliffs.

"There's a ship rounding just there – look - I heard they had two hundred in Hong Kong, but as to what it is now, I cannot tell." Said Mr. Eglinton.

They walked up a short path to Mr. Hammond's hut.

"I beg your pardon, it's not Buckin'am Palace," he said to Martin. "But I do have a little whisky."

Martin drank it. Anything to help with numbing the stench coming from the mounds. The walls of the hut were useless in keeping it out. He noted some hooks with whips on them, thick ropy leather, leg irons, and chains.

Curious about the work, he put down his glass and went outside, drawing closer to the mounds. Seabirds soared above. As he neared a mound where men, at various points, were hacking at the stony mass, he saw a man fall from a height, knocking against several jagged points before he hit the ground.

"I say, a man's fallen!" he ran back to the hut and shouted it in the door. He hurried over to where the body lay still. Oddly, nobody else seemed to bother. The other men continued to work as if nothing had happened, all except one coolie, who left a team gathering the mined guano and came over.

Martin reached the body. The man, clad only in ragged trousers, lay upon his stomach, dead. Martin started back in horror, not so much at the man's injuries, even though he was bleeding from the head, but from the condition of the body that had until a few moments ago, been alive.

He was almost a skeleton. His shoulder blades jutted out, and every bone in his spine was clearly delineated. As bad as that was, his back and shoulders were a mass of scars, some recent and fresh, some older. His wrists and ankles bore scars also.

He glanced back to the hut. Why were they not coming?

The coolie had reached him. Martin was disturbed that he, too, looked starved. Cheekbones jutted from his face and his eyes were hollowed. His back and legs were scarred, and his wrists and ankles bore signs of recent injury. His whole person was dirty.

"Good Lord!" he prayed aloud, looking to the sky at the soaring birds above his head. "What kind of place is this?"

A few other men approached to lift up the body and to take it away. They all had the famished, beaten look. Their eyes held no hope.

Martin rose to his feet.

One of the coolies was watching him.

"Don't you get enough to eat?" he blurted out the question, slapping his stomach. The man began to speak to him in urgent tones, as if pleading for help, gesturing wildly, then clutching his shirt in appeal. He evidently was unaware that Martin was the son of Boss Eglinton.

"I'm sorry," he said, "I'm so sorry – I will do what I can." He hoped he looked sufficiently concerned to give the coolie hope.

He wiped his forehead with his hand. Walking back to the hut, he saw his father coming out of the door.

"You will get used to this," he said. "I intend for you to be based in Peru for a few years. You'll have to make frequent trips out here to make sure Hammond is doing his job. We need to mine as fast as we can, because once the Holy Joes at home find out about this, they'll petition Parliament or write letters to the newspapers. Hammond told me that an English sea captain put in here last week, looked about without as much as a by-your-leave and left again without saying a word. A Bible-thumper, no doubt. Now you've seen the operation, son, so we'll go back."

As they rowed away, a ship came to anchor. Shouts and whips broke the chorus from the birds as dozens of men in irons were shuffled off the ship and into rowing boats.

"How many have we?" shouted Mr. Eglinton across the swathe of water.

"Only eighty three! Dysentery!" was the returning shout.

Martin stared in horror at this father.

"Eighty-three out of two hundred, but it's been worse." Said his father. "There was one time, we lost three quarters."

Martin stared at his father. He did not know this man. He did not know him.

The Eglinton Empire was built on slave labour.

CHAPTER TEN

Martin went straight to his room. His mind was shocked, his senses almost paralysed. The scenes from the miserable island replayed itself over and over. The brutal conditions of the coolies, the death which did not turn a hair of his father's head, the *eighty-three out of two hundred*, not being too bad a loss. The hopelessness he had witnessed. The frantic pleas of the coolie. He drew the bed curtains around him and flung himself on his bed.

A knock came to the door. "Senor Eglinton? Your father is waiting to begin dinner."

He did not reply. The summons was repeated twice more, and then he heard footsteps fading as they went down the hall.

Ten minutes later, the door burst in. His father threw back the bed curtains and glared at him.

"What are you doing, Martin? Did you not hear Carlos knock on the door? He thought you were out. I waited and then decided to see for myself. What's the matter?"

"The mining, Father."

"Oh, you've lost your appetite. That's no reason to be rude! If you didn't want to eat, you should have sent a message. That smell takes getting used to, I suppose it's still in your nostrils."

"Yes Father, it is, but that's not what's sickening me. It's the slaves, Father. The Chinese slaves."

"They aren't slaves. They're indentured. Free to go after their time is up."

Martin sprang to his feet.

"Slavery – indentured – they are captives! The men I saw today looked half-dead, and one of them was dead. Not that you noticed, or cared!" Martin's voice rose as he continued, striding about the room.

"A man died there today and nobody gave a d___! I called to you to come out! Why did you not come? Is it because it's so common an occurrence, or does the sight of a dead emaciated body play on your conscience? Is this what the Eglinton wealth is made of? It's not bird droppings we ought to be ashamed of, Father, it's the blood, sweat, lashings and death! I hate it!"

His father's face was furious.

"How dare you! How dare you speak to me as you do? I've slaved for you, for your mother, your sister! You don't deserve the fine house you grew up in, you don't deserve your schooling, the clothes on your back, your fencing lessons! You're spoiled! Pampered! I'll teach you what it's like to have nothing to your name! You're going to work on that island for the rest of the week. Stripped, the sun on your back, swinging a pickaxe. Then you'll learn that you would much prefer to be rich, to be on our side of wealth instead of the other. It'll teach you *gratitude*. You will thank your lucky stars you were born to a father who knows how to make money.

"How I wish I'd had another son!" he finished, as he banged the door shut behind him.

CHAPTER ELEVEN

Martin took his punishment like a man. At least he provided some amusement for the coolies, as they chuckled about his pale skin, like a ghost, said one who had a little English. He accompanied them, pickaxe in hand, up the stinking mound and began to strike at the rock.

The overseer had orders to treat him like any other man, and he earned his first stripes mid-afternoon, when he thought he would die of thirst, and came a little way to where there was a jug of water on a ledge. He received a burning lash as he hurriedly downed a mouthful.

The coolies began to like him. He had told them his name. They were astonished that the son of Eglinton would work like them. At the end of the day, retiring to a small dormitory hut, they ate a bowl of some indefinable mess and a piece of flat bread, drank dirty water and slept in their clothes.

The second day was worse than the first. Martin's sore muscles began to rebel, but he kept on, gritting his teeth.

Every muscle seemed to be afire. Two men died that day, one from dysentery, and the other from a fall.

On the third day, Martin began to feel ill. It began with a blinding headache before noon, vomiting and an intestinal upset so violent he could hardly move from the latrines. Toward evening, he suffered seizures.

Mr. Hammond called some men to carry him to his own quarters and he laid him on a mat there. Martin fell into unconsciousness.

CHAPTER TWELVE

W hen Martin awoke, he was lying in bed in his room. His father was beside his bed.

"You're awake. Perhaps my punishment was a bit too much. I was angry. You ingested something that infected your brain, the doctor says. Something from the birds. Orni-something. You had seizures."

Martin began to sit up, but when he tried to raise his knees, he could not. He willed his lower limbs to move, but they were like two sticks of wood attached to him. A sickening fear came over him.

"I have no feeling in my legs." he said. "I'm trying to sit up, and I can't get them to move."

"Don't be stupid, Martin, of course you can move your legs."

"I'm telling you, Father, that I have no feeling in my legs at all." Martin stated hotly.

His father gave him a look of annoyance, pulled back the bedclothes and slapped his shin a few times. Martin did not react. Mr. Eglinton reached for his knife and jabbed the sole of his foot. But his son made no instinctive drawing back, no reaction at all, even as a trickle of blood poured from the small cut past his heel and onto the white sheet.

The veins on Mr. Eglinton's neck throbbed and his face paled.

"You must be able to walk. You must be. You can't go home like this. I suppose that the feeling will take a while to come back. Yes, that's what it is."

His father left the room.

The maid, Maria, came in a few minutes later. Her eyes held tears as she helped him to sit up and take some broth. She ministered to him with care, washed the blood from his foot and shook her head in sorrow.

He lay there for hours, thinking. The feeling in his legs would come back, he was sure, so he stopped thinking of that and instead scenes from the island replayed themselves and threatened to overwhelm him. He knew he had witnessed a great evil. An evil unknown to his mother and sister, who were ignorant of what kept them in Clifton Walk, in gowns and jewellery. He guessed that few people in England knew about this; while very aware of the Slave Trade to North America, banned some forty years ago, this had crept up since, stealthily and unremarked. That his own father should be involved was a great betrayal. That he was heir to this enterprise was sickening. He resolved he would never preside over this operation, even if he was cast out on the street.

But perhaps Fate had taken the decision away from him, if he had lost his health. Would the sensation in his legs return? What if it did not? Was he going to be a cripple?

The doctor came to see him that evening. He examined him fully, asked him questions about his sensations, and tested reflexes all over his body with a little hammer. He took his father aside and opined that it was unlikely that his son would ever walk again. The disease had wrought such severe shock upon the system that the spine had been irreparably damaged. It was fortunate, said the doctor, firstly that he had lived, and secondly that he still had the use of his arms and could turn his head.

Mr. Eglinton took it badly. He was filled with a mixture of revulsion for his son and remorse for having been the cause of this catastrophe. He thought that any other lad – the sons of any of his business friends – would not have sickened as his did. Of course, they would not have needed the lesson in gratitude that he had been trying to teach Martin. Phil Carson was out here only two years ago, eighteen years old, he had made no objection to anything he saw, but had taken it all in his stride. His conscience had not been disturbed as Martin's had; his father had not endured a torrent of abuse. He was now overseeing a similar operation on another island. Mr. Carson was to be greatly envied.

Mr. Eglinton concluded that he was not so much the cause of Martin's illness as the boy himself was. His son was sorely lacking.

CHAPTER THIRTEEN

1860

"Penny, the Dalys are in a very bad way at Butlers' Buildings, help me make some broth for them from that old bone, and then we'll mek some pobbies for the children."

Penny had finished the ironing and had taken her candle to her closet to read another chapter of 'Sense *& Sensibility*.' It was hard work reading the interminable sentences and she had to read one to three times to get its meaning. So far she hadn't a great deal of sympathy for the highly-born Dashwood sisters who had fallen low and had to go to live in a cottage. They had the whole cottage and two servants! What were they complaining about?

"Penny!"

"Comin', Mamma." She put the book away with a sigh. When she became rich, nobody would call her to go on a charitable errand. She would help the poor of course, with money, but she would have a cook to make the bone broth and have footmen and maids to take them over to the buildings where the poor lived all crammed together.

A few hours later mother and daughter bent under a low doorway to enter the Daly's dank, foetid room. Penny put her handkerchief to her mouth, but then, realising that she was being rude, took it away and made herself endure the smell. The room was full of sad, immobile figures. The children were listless, and the baby cried as her mother tried to suckle her.

"Mrs. Daly, we've brought some vittles." Said Mrs. Fowler with gentleness. The aroma of food had made the children sit up.

The mother whimpered her thanks, holding out her arms.

"The baby's cryin' cos I have no milk at all," she lamented.

"You will soon, when you've had some food," soothed Mrs. Fowler. "Penny, give the little 'uns their pobbies, afore the milk gets cold."

Soon, Penny was spooning the mush of bread into the hungry mouth of a three-year old who had seated herself on her lap, while her older sisters and brothers helped themselves from the big bowl. She found herself speaking words of encouragement and tenderness to the children, trying to make them smile. The little girl was looking up at her with such gratitude in her eyes that Penny's heart melted. The Fowlers were poor, but the Dalys were destitute. This run-down house was overflowing with Irish families evicted from their poor cabins as their landlords cleared land for pasture after the Potato Famine, and their needs were desperate, far greater than Penny's.

After that, Penny went back several times with a little group that her mother had formed from their parish. For a while, she forgot her aim to become rich. She felt the joy of giving. The gratitude of the emaciated women, and the smiles of the children with full stomachs dropped onto her heart like precious gifts.

On their way home one day, they met Mrs. Foster, a neighbour, who, upon seeing them, crossed the road to meet them. There was an urgency in her manner that alarmed them.

"Penny, don't you as wash for the Eglintons?" she asked.

"Yes, why?"

"Because the young Master has returned from a voyage, paralysed. He can't walk at all, he's a cripple."

Penny and her mother were horrified to hear this. They hurried home to tell Grandma.

"There'll be a lot more to wash," was Grandma's pragmatic response, after she had exclaimed her sorrow and dismay at the young man's misfortune.

More money, thought Penny, before she felt very ashamed of herself for the thought.

CHAPTER FOURTEEN

Mrs. Eglinton threw herself on her knees beside her bed. No greater sorrow had ever visited her than to see Martin come home crippled, unable to help himself. She was numb with anguish. She'd learned it by letter, her husband feeling it better that she get the hysterics over before he arrived, lest he become the target of her wrath. Dr Aldridge and his sister had hurried to her side to comfort her. But for them, and Matilda, she might have fallen very ill.

Weeks of waiting had begun, weeks of hoping, that when Martin arrived, he would be in health. Recovered and in health, and that the predictions of the doctor in Peru would be wrong.

But when she had seen him lifted out of the carriage by two able men, she had almost collapsed in grief. She had struggled to control herself, for his sake, and had taken over his care, bidding the footmen to be careful with him, and to lay him on the couch in the drawing room. There she smothered his face with hugs and kisses. The tears escaped her. Poor Martin had tried to cheer her.

"It's not so bad, Mamma. I can do most things for myself, except walk and run about. I've almost gotten used to it; you will too, in time."

She and Matilda had burst into fresh tears at his efforts to cheer them.

"Oh God," she sobbed now with the heart of a true mother. "Take me instead! Let me die, and give my son back his health!"

No such prayer had ever been thought of by her husband. And the circumstances of Martin's illness would be a secret between him and his son. Martin had come down with a foreign disease in Peru, was all that would be said.

Dr. Aldridge called to see him the following day, and after his examination told his parents that from the examination, it did not appear that the spine had been damaged, therefore he was at a loss to explain what had caused the paralysis, except that whatever bacterium had attacked him, had affected an area of his brain. It was a polio-like illness, but not polio. He had seen a case like it once before, when a housemaid had become very ill from tending a parrot, but it was not so severe as this, and after some months of weakness in every muscle in her body, she had returned to work.

He had also seen, in his practice as a Navy surgeon, patients long confined to bed who had over time suffered muscle loss, and he was emphatic that young Mr. Eglinton should be exercised several times a day to prevent this.

As to whether he would walk again, it was impossible to say.

CHAPTER FIFTEEN

"I was very sorry to hear of young Master's illness, Mrs. Eglinton."

"Thank you, Penny. It's a great cross. To him, and to all who love him too."

"It is not hopeless, I suppose, Mrs. Eglinton. My mother says a person always has to have hope."

"It is only hope that keeps us going sometimes, Penny. But at least he has returned to me, Many do not. I must be grateful for that. There will be more washing, will you manage it, do you think?"

"Why, yes of course, Mrs. Eglinton."

"Thank you. You will be paid extra, of course."

"It's all right, Mrs. Eglinton, really it is." Penny had felt so ashamed of her first thought when she'd heard Grandma declare there'd be more washing that she had determined to refuse more pay, at least at first. She liked Martin and felt genuinely sorry for him. He it was who had told her that she needed to be educated.

"Please tell him that my family wish him very well," she said, upon leaving. "My mother wishes to know if you need any help nursing, that she knows a very good woman."

"Tell your mother I am very grateful for her kindness and her good wishes," said Mrs. Eglinton.

She mounted the stairs to Martin. He spent most of his day upstairs, and sometimes all day. When he wished to come down, two men had to carry him. They had employed a man to attend him. She had purchased a Bath chair and he could be put into it when downstairs, and wheeled about. He could eat with the family and be wheeled out to see the garden.

His world was now very confined. His room, the stairs, the drawing room. The gardens.

She'd noticed, with great pain, how he and his father were to each other. Such coldness! She knew that Mr. Eglinton was seething with silent anger that his son and heir was as good as dead to him with regard to carrying on the business. And Martin blamed his father for his illness. Mary felt that there was more to the story she had been given about what had happened in Peru but she knew it was useless to pry further.

The doorbell rang. As she was passing through the hall, she answered. She was surprised and very pleased to see two old school friends of Martin's come to call upon him. Paul Bell and Albert Rowlands had come a long way and were very anxious to see their old friend. As she brought them upstairs herself and showed them in, arranging chairs by Martin's bedside, she remembered that Albert's father was a renowned doctor, and she resolved to confer with him before he left about the possibility of his father examining Martin. Why should they take the opinion of one doctor in Peru who might, or might not, be skilled? And Dr. Aldridge was so self-effacing, there was not a shred of vanity in him, only a desire to do all he could for his patients that he would not mind at all, she knew, if a second or even a third opinion was obtained.

After lunch, Mrs. Eglinton drew Albert aside and asked him to send his father to see Martin, and Mr. Rowlands said he was sure his father would be very happy to oblige.

CHAPTER SIXTEEN

D r. Rowlands visited two weeks later, and Dr. Aldridge was in attendance also.

Having examined Martin, and spoken at length to him, he narrated his findings to Mrs. Eglinton and Matilda in the drawing room.

"His paralysis is not typical," he said. "I concur with Dr. Aldridge. He has received no injury to cause a paralysis. He has control over bodily functions, which is also not typical in a case of paralysis of the lower limbs due to injury. I would like to call in another specialist, a Dr. Graves."

"And what is his specialty, Dr. Reynolds?"

"His specialty is Psychiatry."

This shocked the two women. There was a stillness in the room.

"You are saying – it's in his mind?" asked Matilda timidly. "He is not – insane, Dr. Rowlands, surely!"

"Insane is not the word I would use. I suspect that the physical shock of his illness, a very severe infection, so affected his mind, that what was supposed to be a temporary paralysis, somehow became extended, and that when the illness subsided, the paralysis should have become resolved, but something is holding it back."

Dr. Aldridge nodded.

"There is hope then, that he will walk again!" cried Mrs. Eglinton.

"I am not so hopeful as all that, Mrs. Eglinton. But allow me to say that it is not a hopeless case. I will write to my colleague directly after returning to Town, and we can both examine your son in consultation with each other."

CHAPTER SEVENTEEN

Mr. Eglinton thought he should return to Manchester for the examination. He was concerned. What he had been doing was illegal for a few years now, and if Martin spilled the beans, there would be no end of trouble. The doctors came and were closeted up with the patient for two hours, and he was not allowed to be present.

"He has symptoms of having suffered a grave shock, such as I have observed in men who have returned from war," said Dr. Graves. "But as to what that was, I cannot say. Men in war have the company of other men, who have been in the same situation as they, to turn to. They may talk to each other of what they had seen and heard and of how they had been injured. But as to this case – I really am at a loss as to what to say. He would not admit to any assault, any accident, any disturbance, other than he got too hot one day, and perhaps drank some bad water, and from that incurred the infection which nearly finished him."

"Is he malingering?" asked his father with bluntness.

"Certainly not. His reflexes are absent. Even the toughest athlete, with the greatest self-control, could not but flinch even a little at the rigourous examination we have conducted. His lower limbs do not respond to touch, nor to painful stimuli."

Nothing was resolved and Mrs. Eglinton wept again. The doctors could not give much hope.

CHAPTER EIGHTEEN

Martin could pull his legs up toward him, with his hands, one by one, and rub the calves to stimulate them. Dr. Aldridge was most particular about that. He had nothing much else to do all day, and the doctors' words had frightened him. He hoped to walk again, and if it helped to exercise his leg muscles, that he would do. He devised other movements for his feet and toes, using his hands, and lengths of ropes and slings. He was determined that if sensation returned that he would be ready.

Dr. Graves, the Psychiatrist, had asked him many probing questions about his voyage, about the events preceding the onset of illness, which he ably deflected. He had no wish to revisit the scenes of his distress. He had put it away, in a little locked room in his mind, and there it would stay. He would forget about it. It could not and must not be mentioned. His father was somehow getting around the law which mandated decent living conditions for every ship leaving Hong Kong. As for the mining, there was only a certain supply of guano to be got from the mounds, and his father was hurrying to get as much as he could before it was exhausted. He planned then to go into the business of transporting textiles between England and the Americas, but knowing his father well, Martin had no doubt that he would cheat to improve his own profit margin.

The family business disgusted him. His father's way of making money was repugnant to him.

His father left for another voyage; autumn came in, and winter and spring came and left without any change in his condition. His mood had become more quiet and sad as his crippled condition became more of a reality for him. His friends soon forgot him – though he would have liked to hear of their house parties and hunts and travels, some felt that he was better off not knowing about their good times when he could not share in them, and others forgot him altogether.

He knew every detail of his room. He knew every curve of every piece of wood, every leaf on the ferny wallpaper. Every fold in the curtains was the same. Mornings saw Benjamin, his man, come in and give him breakfast and help him to the water closet. After breakfast he sat out while the maids made his bed and dusted the room. He sat by the window and saw the front garden. His mother had planted colourful shrubs in his view. He saw the dog romp about. On Thursdays, he saw Penny let herself in the gate, hamper on her hip, and make her way around the side of the house. He began to watch for Penny on Thursdays, and note the time of her arrival, and become concerned if she was late. He knew she walked along the railway line, but he did not see a companion. His mother told him of the other girl who walked with her, so he was satisfied. Penny had a firm, decisive step, and she cut a pretty figure with the hamper on her hip. Sometimes she paused and seemed to look up at the house, as if examining it. He drew his head back a little so he would not be seen looking at her. Sometimes, she came on Fridays instead of Thursdays, and those Thursdays, he was disappointed, as if something had been missing from his day. But watching for her the following day cheered him again.

Some mornings, he was carried downstairs by Benjamin and the gardener, and put into his Bath chair. In the drawing room, his mother tried to amuse him to the point of exasperation.

"Martin, I procured 'Little Dorrit' by Charles Dickens, it's charming, I'm sure you will love it."

"I'm tired of reading, Mother."

"Here is a book of poetry by the American Emily Dickinson."

"She writes too much about death."

"I shall ask Benjamin to amuse you with chess."

"Mother, Benjamin is no good at chess. He gives me no challenge at all."

"Matilda can read to you, if you are too tired to read."

"Matilda has no time. She's getting ready to go to the Valleys house party. Let her be. At least one of us should have a good life."

"A game of cards, Martin?" she asked one day, taking out the deck.

"All right, Mother. If you like."

"You're only playing to please me, then?"

"Yes, rather."

"Martin, you're impossible! I don't know how you can just sit and mope all day! You have no interest in anything at all, you're bored and unhappy, and yet, won't help yourself. It makes your situation harder for all of us! Your bitterness and sharpness of manner is hurting everybody. Did you have to snap at Matilda this morning, because she asked you if you wished William Valley to come over and amuse you with a few songs?"

She stormed out of the room. Martin looked at his useless legs. He pummelled them, but felt nothing, nothing at all; they were dead.

William Valley came over anyway, because it was an excuse to see Matilda. She had grown very tall, which left her rather a wallflower at dances and assemblies, as shorter men were not keen to be seen standing up next to her. Her father told she would have trouble finding a husband because men did not like to look up to their wives. But William Valley, who was just her own height of five feet ten inches, admired her enormously. He began to pay calls and before long, they were in love and engaged.

CHAPTER NINETEEN

On a fine summer morning, Penny entered the Eglinton gate, and saw Martin sitting out on the porch. He had seen her, and waved. She waved back. He beckoned. She walked steadily over to him and set her hamper outside on the grass.

"Master Eglinton, it's good to see you. You're looking well." It was a fib, but one said that to invalids.

Martin laughed. "No, I'm not, but thank you just the same. I haven't talked to you for a long time. How is everything with you?"

"Very well, thank you."

"Are you still reading?"

"Yes. I still like reading. Miss Villiers, a teacher – " (she stopped herself from saying *'at the Ragged School'*) " – borrows books for me from the library, and there are a few bookshops I like to go to sometimes, to buy books."

"Are you going to become a governess, is that it?"

"Oh no, I'm not as educated as all that," she said with regret. She knew that to become a governess, she would have to have French, and History and Geography and other subjects she knew nothing of. She knew now that she might never become rich. It was a bitter pill. "I don't have much education at all, really, apart from reading, but books do take me to different places, inside of England and outside of England, and to other times in History as well."

"Well you see the way I am," he said. "I'd give my entire education to be able to walk again."

"It is very unfortunate," she said.

"I say, Penny, would it be – an imposition for you to read to me sometime? I would love to hear you read."

A smile stole across Penny's face.

"What would your mother say to that?" she asked, wondering if this would be something she would be paid for, or whether she would be expected to do it free.

"I'm sure she would agree. I shall ask her tonight. And if you had time, on Thursdays, to spend an hour or two – I would be so grateful."

Penny wondered how much she should get for this occupation. As if reading her mind, Martin smiled.

"Mother will pay you, half a crown maybe, for an hour. How does that sound?"

Penny was flabbergasted. To do something she loved to do for two and sixpence an hour?

"But I walk with a friend, however, she can wait for me." She said quickly. She would not allow Betty to spoil this opportunity for her.

"I daresay Mother may find something for her to do also, some little occupation for an hour or so. I have heard her say that she wants someone to help her with bits and pieces of sewing. She was going to send it out, but perhaps your friend can do it."

"I had better be getting on, Master Eglinton. Shall we begin next Thursday?"

"Next Thursday it shall be."

Penny took up her basket again and walked to the kitchen.

Where would she read to him? Perhaps the drawing room, or his own room. It did not matter, she was going to see the inside of the house again. She looked forward to that very much.

Martin's mood lightened immediately. He now had more to look forward to on Thursdays than seeing Penny come in the gate and leave again soon afterward.

CHAPTER TWENTY

"He wants you to read to him, for half-a-crown? That's very generous of 'im." Said Mrs. Fowler. "Are you sure you'll be good enough with all them long words in the books?"

"I can read very well," said Penny proudly. "I don't know what 'e wants me to read, yet, but I'm sure I'll manage it."

"An hour's readin would be quite enough for me," said Mrs. Pyke. "When you read to us 'ere, tho' it's very pretty readin', I can go to sleep, not that you don't 'ave a nice voice an' all, but there you are. If Master Eglinton 'as the use of hands and eyes, why does 'e want you to read to 'im? I suppose you can't come to any 'arm from an invalid, but don't perform any other service for 'im. It wouldna be decent."

"Grandma!"

"You'll 'ave to dress up a bit, if you're going to be in the 'ouse," said Mrs. Fowler. Penny had been thinking exactly the same thing. She bought a new shawl, a lilac wool and silk mix with fringes, called *barege*, pretty but not too fancy, as befitted her station.

The following Thursday after delivering the linen, she went to the patio where Martin sat at a table with a selection of books on it. He invited her to sit down. He wanted her to read *'Gulliver's Travels.'.*

Penny thought it a very odd book, but interesting in its way. Martin let her read on for about ten minutes, but then began to gently interrupt her to correct pronunciation.

"You don't mind, do you, Penny? You're not offended? You're reading very well, at just the right pace, but if you mind my correcting your pronunciation, I won't."

"I'm not offended – I would be grateful to be corrected," Penny said hastily. She wanted to be able to pronounce words correctly.

Half-an-hour later, Penny was very surprised to see a maid bring a tray of tea. The silver tray was covered with a white cloth, one with which she was very familiar, as she'd often washed, ironed and starched it. The crockery was bone china, and the milk-jug and sugar-bowl matched. Penny had never seen anything so dainty. She remembered every detail to regale at home.

"We shall leave off for a few minutes," Martin said. "I hope you like macaroons."

Macaroons! She'd had one once, when a Lady had brought them to the Ragged School for a Christmas treat.

They resumed their reading after finishing their tea, and the tray had been taken away. Mrs. Eglinton came and thanked her before she left, and she walked away with her half-crown hot in her palm.

CHAPTER TWENTY-ONE

The reading went on for the remainder of the summer, and they moved indoors as the days began to cool. Martin did not always want her to read, though. One day he produced a chessboard and asked if he could teach her chess, as he so enjoyed a game.

Those games went on longer than an hour, and Penny was paid for as long as she was there. Martin was a patient teacher. By November, Penny was a competent opponent. She was a fast learner. The first time she called 'Checkmate!' was a triumph for her, as Martin's King was hopelessly surrounded. He grinned from ear to ear, shaking his head.

Mrs. Eglinton was present, sewing and watching. She seemed to be present a great deal of the time now, and made pleasant conversation with Penny. As always, the tea appeared like clockwork, served on an elegant tray. Sometimes there was cake, sometimes tarts, or a selection of fine biscuits.

Betty was glad of the extra work as well, although she was only getting a shilling an hour. Penny did not tell her how much she was earning.

One day, it was getting on for one o'clock, and Martin had won this time, and Penny thought it was high time she was getting back.

"You must stay and have lunch with us today," said Mrs. Eglinton.

"Lunch? Here?"

"Yes, here, why not? I had Millie set the table for three." Matilda, married now, had moved to her husband's home about two miles away.

"And Betty may have her lunch here too. Cook has set a place for her at the table downstairs."

Penny wondered if she was dreaming. She immediately felt that she was not dressed properly, or that her table manners would be very much lacking. But not for a moment did she consider a refusal, even though her humble jam sandwich waited, tucked away in a little bag.

She followed Mrs. Eglinton into the dining room. She remembered the long table, now covered with a white tablecloth – again, a familiar object to her.

The footman, Hynes, after wheeling Martin in to the table and putting cushions behind him to make him more upright, pulled out a chair for her. In front of her was a place setting fit for Royalty. So many forks and knives and spoons!

"This tablecloth," she said chattily in her nervousness, "Is this the one that had that stubborn blackberry stain?"

"Yes, it is the very one!" said Mrs. Eglinton. "You are quick, Penny! It never really came out, did it? It set for too long before I gave it to you. Look, I cover it with the sugar bowl!"

A door opened, and an aroma announced the food, brought in by Millie and Hynes on platters covered with large silver bowls. She fell silent as each dish was revealed and looked with anxiety at her cutlery. How would she know what to use?

She followed them in their choosing which spoon to use for the soup, which knife to butter her bread with, and which fork to use to eat the roast lamb and potatoes and carrots put before her. She had never feasted like this in all her life. She sat straight; her mother had never allowed her to slump. She had a chocolate mousse with cream afterward, and a cup of coffee with real cream. She'd never tasted coffee and did not like it, so she helped herself to even more cream to mask the taste.

She tried to refuse the extra half-crown Mrs. Eglinton was pressing upon her as she left soon after. It wasn't right to take it, she felt. Not after that sumptuous lunch. She was flabbergasted. But her hostess insisted.

Betty was all chatter on the way home. She too had had a fine dinner of meat and gravy and potatoes and apple tart and tea afterwards. She did not resent at all that Penny had eaten upstairs.

Penny wondered why they were giving her singular attention. It was almost as if she were being *courted*. *Courted!*

No, surely not. They could not have that in mind. It was simply a courtesy for being so obliging to Martin. They were grateful that she was good company for him. But how wonderful it would be to be rich, and to eat like that every day of your life!

CHAPTER TWENTY-TWO

"What do you think, Martin?"

"I really don't know, Mother. Since Penny's visits began, I've found a reason to get up every morning. Even though she's only here on Thursdays, that day is so much brighter, so much better. Penny learns so quickly, that in a few years, nobody will be able to tell that she was not born into the upper class, which is what they are beginning to call us successful industrialists, isn't it? She is very willing to be corrected, to learn the better way of doing and saying. But on the other hand – it would not be just. No, it cannot be, Mother, it cannot be. I'm a cripple. Who wants to marry someone who cannot walk? And then there's - "he stopped, avoiding his mother's eye.

"The begetting?" said his mother, rather clumsily, but she did not know how to put it.

"Yes. What kind of husband would I be? Although Dr. Aldridge says I might - beget." He said no more on the delicate subject, but he had complete control over personal body functions.

But Mrs. Eglinton saw a bigger problem. Mr. Eglinton would never suffer his family to undergo the indignity of marriage to a lowly washerwoman from Manchester's slums. Even though Martin ceased to think of marrying Penny, and was content to have her visit weekly indefinitely, his mother persisted in her quest. Her fear was that Penny would get married or move away, and her son would be bereft. She must not allow Penny to escape.

"But does she love him, Mamma?" asked Matilda, now a very happy Mrs. Valley, when Mrs Eglinton called to her one fine day in May to discuss the matter. Matilda was sewing a long white gown for her first child, expected soon.

"She seems happy in his company, and why should she not love him?" Mrs. Eglinton seemed a little defensive, as if anybody could not love her son.

"If she were to consent, it will just be for the money! She's a laundress. An offer like this would be irresistible." Matilda rummaged in her basket for some lace.

"But she is not in the general run of maids, Matilda. In her mind, she's above it. She reads very well, you know."

Matilda frowned. Her mother was determined to see all that she wished to see. It was because she loved her son, of course. But Matilda, who loved her brother also, was troubled by what her mother refused to see.

"I have nothing against Penny Fowler. And if she were to make Martin's life better, that would make everybody so happy. But her family, Mamma – the connection!"

Mrs. Eglinton waved that aside.

"What does it matter? Your grandfather was a struggling tradesman. Now that's an end to it. Matilda, don't add lace to the cuffs, it looks very dainty but he will catch his little fingers in it."

CHAPTER TWENTY-THREE

I t was getting on close to five o'clock, and there was no sign of Penny on this bright June evening.

"There's something going on out there, I tell you, Emma. All this playing of chess and other things, and readin', young Mr. Eglinton is falling in love with her and will make her an offer. Stayin' *'to lunch'*, they call it! Instead of dinner, like good honest folks. There was no lunches when I was young. We fasted from breakfast to dinner. And what did she bring 'ome last week? A side of beef! And a bag of apples they'd stored all the winter, the week afore that! What are they up to?"

"They're just grateful, Mother. They like her and want to treat her well."

"Who do you think they will get to marry young Mr. Eglinton?"

"Invalids don't marry, generally speaking. The Church don't allow it. Marriage is for children and they can't beget."

"I tell you, child, that our Penelope will get an offer, soon. Maybe it's happened already. Today!"

"If she did, I hope she refused." Mrs. Fowler said. "For I'm sure my Penny doesn't love young Mr. Eglinton and I wouldn't like her to accept just 'cos she'd be rich, like."

"I beg ter disagree with you. She should do the best she can for 'erself. And she can't do better than Martin Eglinton. Look! That's 'er passin' the window!"

The door pushed open and Penny entered. She put the hamper of dirty linen down on the floor and said:

"Well tha' won't last much longer! But don't ye worry, ye'll be well looked-after!"

"I told you 'ow it would be," said Grandma to Mrs. Fowler, with triumph.

"I'm gettin' married," announced Penny. "This time next month, I'll be Mrs. Martin Eglinton. Fancy that!"

CHAPTER TWENTY-FOUR

Penny sat down and told them all. Mrs. Eglinton it was that had broached the subject, out in the garden where she had been asked to walk with her. She'd said that her son was in love with her, but feeling he had not his health to offer, was not inclined to ask for her hand. So, she wanted to know if Penny would be averse to an offer from Martin, or in favour.

"I told her I'd be in favour," Penny said proudly. "There now! I'll be rich."

"You're not even lettin' on to be in love with him!" cried her horrified mother. "All you can think of, is the money, the gowns, the jewels! I'm reet ashamed of you, Penelope Fowler!"

"The match suits them as it suits me," Penny said with complacency. "He knows I don't love him. He doesna mind, he said *'Love will come.'* And Mamma, as you've called me *Penelope*, that's what I want to be known as. No more *Penny*."

"What 'is father goin' to say?" demanded her mother.

"Well I don't know. That I don't care about. Martin says we have to be married afore he comes home, so he can't stop us. Martin is of age to do anything he pleases." Penny took up the hamper and brought it into the back-kitchen.

"No more washin' of other people's linen, nor even of my own!" she said happily, dancing about the living room when she came out again.

CHAPTER TWENTY-FIVE

Penny became Mrs. Eglinton three weeks later. She had spent the last week before the wedding at Eglinton House in Matilda's old room. Lying there on her first night, she'd remembered how awestruck she had been at the age of seven, when she had beheld it for the first time. Now she was to be the young Mistress!

They were married in the drawing room of Eglinton House, with just a few guests to a fine breakfast afterwards. Grandma and Mrs. Fowler attended, though the latter disapproved of Penny's reason for marrying, she wished her daughter very happy, and both wanted to meet the groom and his family. He appeared to her to be a very good sort of man, not much fire about him, but steady and quiet. He was just the type of man to suit Penny but not the sort to be able to persuade her from owt she wished to do. But this was a different kind of marriage from the normal. She hoped that her daughter would take her vows seriously, for love, honour and obey was a tall order when she neither loved him nor honoured him at the outset. Martin would not probably not demand obedience, she knew. *'In sickness and in health, till death us do part.'* She hoped that Penny meant that.

They were dressed as well as they could, by borrowing the best from neighbours and friends, and were made much of by Martin and his mother and family. Penny was very keen that they enjoy everything and made sure they tasted all of the fine fare put before them, and they went home as they had come, in a hired cab paid for by the Eglintons.

Besides her family, there were only the Aldridges and Mr. and Mrs. Valley there. Martin held her hand tightly whenever he could, and kissed her ardently when they were alone. She responded to him, but knew there would be no relations. Her mother had told her bluntly what the situation should be between married people, and that it would not be so for her. She'd had second thoughts at the prospect of having no children, but she could not give up the chance for an easy life for the rest of her days. Martin Eglinton was her ambition handed to her, on a silver platter!

'I am rich, I am rich!' she sang quietly to herself as she made herself ready for bed on her wedding night. Her room was next to her husband's. It was painted yellow and white, colours she had chosen herself. She was to attend a dressmakers in the morning with her mother-in-law, to be measured for a wardrobe befitting her station. Mrs. Eglinton had also bestowed some of her own jewellery upon her, and Martin had sent off to Town for a sparkling diamond wedding band and other pieces she could only have dreamed of in the past. She needed yards of material for summer gowns and petticoats, she needed boots and shoes, parasols, several pairs of gloves without which a Lady could not be seen, and she wished to hide her hands. She needed hats, bonnets, shawls, ribbons, lace to make collars and cuffs, netting, combs, writing paper, pens and many other sundries.

Should she think about her winter clothes also? Wool for winter gowns and a warm hooded cloak, and a muff. She had procured for herself, before her wedding, a catalogue from Kendal, Milne & Faulkner and ordered freely from it. Mrs. Eglinton was taken aback at the size of her order, but Martin insisted she have everything she wanted, and it just showed how well she could adapt, she had a sense of her new rank and situation.

As for him, he awoke the first morning after their wedding, and had the happy thought that Penny was his wife. But this was followed by the stark realisation that they may forever be in separate beds. He pulled himself up suddenly as best he could, and became determined to walk again, even if it took all of his effort. He began to think deeply. What would help him?

How could he employ his brain to serve his legs?

When Benjamin came in, he said: "I want you to call in a carpenter. I wish to meet with him. I'm going to need some items built for me."

Penny came in to bid her husband good morning. She was dressed in one of Matilda's cut-down dresses and looked very happy. During the morning, she busied herself going about the rooms, examining each corner of her new home, until her mother-in-law wondered if she was planning to become the Mistress of it sooner rather than later. She was in good health, and still young, she had no intention of giving way!

But Mrs. Eglinton had to worry about a letter she had to write, to Mr. Eglinton. It was better to let him know about Martin's marriage by letter. Let him get his seethings and tantrums over before he reached England. She knew she did not want to be near him when he heard of it. She went to her

84

desk in the morning room where she attended to all her correspondence, and agonised over the letter, discarding one sheet of paper after another. Finally she decided on simply writing:

Dearest Henry,

I have news that you may not like to hear. Martin is married since July 5th. The bride is a Miss Penelope Fowler, a Manchester girl born and bred. Her father is deceased this long time. Her mother and grandmother are known to us, but perhaps you do not remember them. We had a private ceremony in Eglinton House with just Family present. Rev. Sherlock did the offices. Penelope is a good companion for our son in his miserable illness, and he is very fond of her. You will meet her when you return. We are all well, and Matilda expects to be confined in the next few weeks.

Your loving wife

Mary

CHAPTER TWENTY-SIX

The parcels arrived one after another, and were unpacked in great excitement, with Martin present, as he wished to see Penny's face light up in delight at each purchase. He was happier by the day, as was Penny. She dressed as an elegant lady now. She loved her new clothes and jewellery, and soon longed to have a ballgown. Not that she had any plans to attend a ball, but just in case? Duchess satin, or silk georgette? What colour? An overskirt or not? And what about a headpiece?

"Martin, put a stop to this spending," implored his mother. "She will have us in the Workhouse!"

"Oh Mother, allow her to have her head. She's had nothing all her life."

"We're running up high bills everywhere. And she ordered a cheval mirror too. The one already in the room is not good enough! When your father comes, he will become very angry."

They did not have very long to wait for Mr. Eglinton's arrival, for as soon as he received the letter handed to him in

Port Elizabeth in South Africa, and read its contents, he set out for England. He fumed all the way. He of course knew who the Fowlers were! He knew from the account books. There was a Mrs. Pyke a laundress, who was succeeded by a Miss P. Fowler. A washerwoman to be mistress-in-waiting at Eglinton House! The hussy. The scheming little jade. He would send her packing. But he supposed that she'd have to be paid off. Why had none of his family any common sense?

CHAPTER TWENTY-SEVEN

The neighbourhood was very curious about the new Mrs. Eglinton and they trooped by in a steady stream of visits to take a view of the bride. Her background was well-known, there was no point in hiding it, as the servants had spread the news, pleased for the most part that one of them had '*made good*'. In their hopeful hearts, if it were possible for Penny Fowler, it may be possible for any of them, though the more cynical said that she only did it for the money.

Penny sat in the drawing room in her new finery, smiling and appearing to enjoy herself, but in reality she was very bored, and rather annoyed at the stares when visitors thought she was not looking. In the normal way she and Martin should return these visits but that was not expected, so Mrs. Eglinton proposed that she go in his stead. Penny looked forward to returning the visits. She longed to see the inside of other peoples' houses. She had formed plans for the redecoration of Eglinton House in her taste, but it would have to wait, she thought regretfully, until she was the actual mistress. And Mrs. Eglinton looked healthy as a horse.

She sat and drank from dainty teacups, and in the middle of one afternoon tea visit, in a house where the conversation was boring and the hostess insipid, she began to long to go back to see her mother and grandmother. It struck her too, with shame, that she had not invited them to come to her. How could she have been so remiss, so involved in her own affairs that her kin was forgotten to her? She decided to go to Red Bank the following day and deliver an invitation. It also pleased her that her old neighbours would see her in her new clothes, stepping out of a hackney in Regents Court.

CHAPTER TWENTY-EIGHT

"Here we are!" The cabman did not know what had brought this lady in fine silk down to this area of Manchester, some charitable work maybe? Or some ill-gotten profit from rakes in high-born families? She tipped him generously. He gave her the benefit of the doubt.

She opened the door and walked in. Her mother was darning her old plaid shawl, and the room was cold, though it was only September. It seemed much smaller than she remembered. How had she ever lived here?

They rose to welcome her and took her silk shawl, admiring it and arranging it carefully on the back of a chair, and she sat down by the table.

"Are you happy, Penny?" asked Grandma from her place by the chimney-piece, though no fire burned there.

"Oh yes, happier than I ever thought I could be!" was the reply. "I've been visiting all the neighbours around, and such houses you never saw in your life! The de Clares have a marble fireplace that came all the way from Italy, and Colonel Brinkley made a fortune in Antigua, he has all kinds of trophies, but best of all, the Butlers intend to give a Ball in honour of their cousin home from India – what's the matter, Mamma? Why are you looking at me like that?"

"How is young Mr. Eglinton?" asked Mrs. Fowler with a very deliberate tone.

"Why, he is very well. He can't come on the visits of course, Mrs. Eglinton accompanies me. Do you see my hat-pin? She gave it to me, it belonged to Martin's grandmother. And a pair of beige lace gloves, but I don't like those so much, so I brought them, would you like them, Mamma?"

"No, thank you."

"What's wrong? Why do I feel unwelcome?"

"Because you haven't asked as to how we are, only to come in and brag and boast of all you have now."

"Leave 'er alone, Emma."

"I will not. Sometimes Love has to speak unwelcome truths. Penny, your 'ead has been turned, and it's not a good thing. You'll never be 'appy if you think only of yourself."

"Will you drink tea with us, Penny?" asked Grandma.

"I'd love a cup." Penny said, ignoring that Grandma had called her '*Penny*' twice now. It was difficult to change even Martin and his mother to call her *Penelope*, so she was resigned.

The cups and saucers were put out, the saucers cracked here and there on their edges, the cups brown around the rims. Penny was about to tell them about the Wedgewood china that was got out for visitors in Eglinton House, but thought better of it. The tea tasted bitter. It was a cheap brand and she'd gotten used to the best. Her mother cut a piece of old fruit cake that was kept in a tin.

"Look, the neighbours are comin' to see you," Grandma noticed the figures pass the window, and sure enough, another moment and two women and three little girls were in the house.

"We come to pay our respects to Mrs. Eglinton," they said, and stared at her, taking in every little detail they could, to recount to those unlucky enough to miss the spectacle. Word spread, and soon the room was full. Penny felt like the Queen. Gradually, they left again, and she rose to leave.

"I came to deliver an invitation to lunch," she said. "You will come, won't you, Mother? Don't tell me as I'm a stranger to you now, you 'ave not been nice to me since I came in, and I don't want us to quarrel. Look, I 'ave some money for you." She laid a purse on the table.

"Take it back," said Mrs. Fowler. "I don't like the way you got it." She was back to darning, and snapped the thread with her teeth.

"Emma," her grandmother reproached her own daughter. "That's very uncivil, it is. I'll take it, if you won't. I could use some liniment for my old bones for the winter. Thank you, Penny."

"Thank you Grandmamma." Penny felt close to tears. "Mamma, say you will come to lunch, please? On a Sunday, when you're off?"

"I will come," she said. "Daughter, don't let riches go to your 'ead, I beg you. Never forget where you came from. Remember Job. He had everything, and it was all gone."

"But he got it all back, Mamma," Penny said cheerily.

"And never forget those who have nothing, who are worse off even than us."

Penny remembered the resolution she had often made to herself, that if she ever became rich, she'd help the poor. She thought of the Daly family, and the other destitute families crowding into the small dingy rooms.

"I will help the poor, Mamma. I will," she said. Her mother embraced her and she left, with a little crowd of children following her until she gained the street from where she could hail a passing hackney. She gave the children a penny each for sweets before she got in. As the carriage left her old neighbourhood behind, she felt suddenly lonely. She was above them now, and it would never be the same. She wiped a tear from her eye, and then cheered up. The Ball! Martin would not mind her going, she was sure.

When she reached Eglinton House, she knew something had happened while she was out. There was a tension in the air, the servants were scurrying around, and she saw a strange hat and coat upon the hallstand.

"Is that her?" bellowed a male voice from upstairs, and the beanpole middle-aged man descended hurriedly. He looked quite angry. She steeled herself. Mr. Eglinton!

CHAPTER TWENTY-NINE

Her mother-in-law appeared in the hall. She seemed nervous, and twisted her hands.

"My dear, this is Penelope."

"So I guessed." He looked at her coldly.

"You are Martin's father." she said.

"Yes, I am. And I have his interests at heart. Unlike you."

"I beg your pardon!"

"There's no use in begging my pardon. Come, let us speak in my study. You come too, Mary."

He shut the door when all three were inside.

"How much?" he asked Penny, abruptly turning to her.

"What do you mean?" she asked.

"How much money do you want?"

"I don't want money!" she said, hotly.

"Of course you do, that's why you're here." He said smoothly. "I would have done the same, if I were you. An offer you couldn't refuse, eh?"

"How dare you insult me!"

"I'm not insulting you, unless I were to insult myself. I'm a very practical man, and I told you I would have done the same, had I been a pretty little woman with no money, and a great offer was made to me, far above my station. It was very clever, but I won't have it, because this is my family. How much do you want to make you leave this house and never return?"

"You'd break your own son's 'eart, to satisfy yourself?" snapped Penny.

"You see! I told you she loved him!" cried Mary with relieved triumph.

"Do you? *Love!* Do you love him?" Mr. Eglinton was looking at her, with a smirk.

"Of course I love 'im!" she said. It felt like a lie, and yet there was a little stirring in her heart, a flicker of affection that rose in indignation at the injustice and callousness of his father toward him.

"You are a pretty little liar, too."

The flicker rose into a flame.

"He doesn't deserve a parent like you that I know."

"Oh, Penny." Mrs. Eglinton covered her eyes with both hands.

"Why? Why do you say that?" he looked at her, suddenly suspiciously. His eyes flickered, from her to his wife and back again.

"Because you want to take away 'is happiness," she said.

A shout reached them.

"What are you all talking about? If you want to discuss me, I would far rather it was in my presence!" Martin's angry voice carried from his room down the hall.

They rose immediately to go to him.

"Oh Martin," cried Penny, when she saw him. He had tried to get out of his chair, and was sprawled upon the floor. Penny knelt by him and shouted for Benjamin.

CHAPTER THIRTY

Penny could not sleep. That Mr. Eglinton could see through her so easily was disturbing. He was a dreadful man, an unpleasant, greedy man. She was not like him of course. She'd married Martin to get out of her own poverty; that wasn't greedy. That was doing the best you could for yourself. It was about surviving. No, Penny, she said to herself, tossing, you wanted to be rich. You didn't want enough, you wanted more than enough.

She felt pangs of guilt.

But she'd made Martin happy! He loved her, and she was his wife, and would be with him always.

Always? The thought unsettled her, and she turned again. But – he would not live that long, would he? Invalids died young.

You wicked woman, she said to herself for having such a thought.

This was the devil, she knew, tempting her to wish poor Martin away! The darkness of the room seemed to envelop her in bleak, evil thoughts. She sat up and lit a candle.

She would be a good, devoted wife to Martin Eglinton. She would ask for nothing, except her gowns and jewels and fine cuisine. She would be content with that.

But as she knew she could not.

She got out of bed and knelt by her bed, praying for she knew not what, only she wanted to become a good, loving person who was not greedy.

Mr. Eglinton ignored her the following day. Perhaps Martin had spoken strongly to him.

She was very devoted to Martin that day, and joined him in the drawing room after he had been brought down and settled in an armchair. Dr. Aldridge had warned him not to sit all day in the Bath chair, it was for transport, not for sitting all day in.

"Shall we have a game of chess?" she asked him.

"Oh, have you time? No dress fittings this morning?" he asked, a little pointedly, but with humour.

"No, nothing at all. I have been so busy organising my clothes, choosing and buying, over the last few months. Martin, my changed situation went to my head a little. I haven't paid you enough attention. You have been so generous." She placed her hand on his.

"You are the generous one," he said, taking her hand to his lips. She wanted to draw closer to him, but he laid her hand down. "Come, get the board, I intend to give you the game of your life."

But Martin was not in humour, she could see. Was it the fall yesterday? He had not broken anything, but it was distressing to have wanted to walk so much, to have made a useless attempt and to have to have been picked up off the floor. Was it the annoyance at being talked about or the fury at what his father had tried to do? He had not said how much he had heard.

"You're not in your usual fighting form," she said, as she checkmated his King only forty-five minutes later. "What is it?"

"Oh, everything," he said with vagueness. "But something in particular."

"What is that?"

"The doctor said that my paralysis may be due to a shock received to my mind, or something, and that my body, when it became ill, could not recover completely due to this shock."

"What was the shock, Martin?"

"I cannot speak of it. Do you know, Penny, I have had a carpenter fashion some frames for me, so that I may get about my room by the strength of my hands, leaning on them. I have had Benjamin walk behind me, to hold me up. So far, there is no success; my feet drag. Useless things! But I'm not giving up. I want to walk again, and I want us to be husband and wife."

He looked at her with such love in his eyes that she felt guilty at her own thoughts of the night before, the terrible temptation that she wanted it all for herself.

CHAPTER THIRTY-ONE

There was a moratorium on her spending, imposed by her father-in-law. Luckily she had already ordered the marigold-yellow duchesse satin and white tulle for her ballgown, and as soon as it arrived she made sure to hurry it to the dressmakers to be cut out, so that it could not be sent back. She was very pleased that when the bill came, she was able to tell him that it was too late, the gown was cut up and halfway made. He looked at her, speechless.

"If you were a man, I'd call you out," he said to her across the breakfast table, looking out over his glasses. "Or, maybe I would take you on as my business partner."

She did not take this last as a compliment. Thankfully he went to Liverpool, and from there to Exeter and Bristol, and only spent a few days at home again before setting off for another part of the world. While he was in Liverpool, her mother and grandmother came on their planned visit, and she was very relieved that he was not there to spoil the company.

"If you think I have finished with this matter of your marriage to my son, you are mistaken." he warned Penny before he left. They were alone in the drawing room at the time. "I will give you one more chance. Five hundred pounds to leave this house. I warn you, if you love Martin as you say, you will take it and never come back."

"I refuse."

"Very well. Be it upon your own head."

Afterwards, Penny wondered that if he had offered her five hundred pounds as an annuity, might she have accepted it? The thought made her uncomfortable, because she would have at least hesitated. That would have been tempting indeed.

The house itself seemed to sigh with relief when Mr. Eglinton left. As the colder weather came, Penny was keeping her resolution of spending time with Martin. But he seemed sad, and sometimes bitter, and often would not talk at all. He was dragging himself around his room daily with Benjamin's help, and so far, there was no improvement.

The much expected invitation from the Butlers came at last! Inviting all of them, of course, but Martin could not attend.

"You may go if you wish," he said to her. "With Mother, I think she would like to go also."

Penny wondered if Dr. Aldridge would be there. When Mr. Eglinton was away, his professional visits to Martin were followed by a chat with his mother in the drawing room, but when his father was at home, he left immediately. She saw that Mrs. Eglinton took care never to mention his name. To her, all of that looked a little suspicious. Were they in love?

Her marigold-yellow gown was made up, with its ruffled bodice, short white lacy sleeves and a flounced skirt trimmed with white silk bows. She shimmered with every movement. The dressmaker, with whom she was on excellent terms, had procured a special pattern from Paris and said that she was the only lady she was making this style for. She loved her long white gloves. She was still conscious of her hands – they had not lost their working-woman look. She wore a pearl necklace which had belonged to Martin's grandmother.

Millie helped her to dress and arrange her hair, and she went into Martin's room to show herself to him before she left. "You look simply beautiful," he said with obvious wistfulness. "Come closer, so I can see the arrangement on your hair a little better. Nosegays and nettings and ribbons! How I would love to go with you, and dance – perhaps someday, Penny. Did you put on the perfume I ordered for you? Yes, I can smell it. Frangipanni, from John Gosnell's Perfumery. You must tell me about the Ball when you come back. I shall be awake." He pressed her hand warmly.

She kissed him and left, and his evening, alone in the house, would be spent reading by the light of a candle.

The Butler home was a large late Georgian building, neatly laid out in a small park. The carriages turned at a sweep in front of the main door, and Penny had never seen so much fashion and style as she saw emerging from them. It seems nearly every young lady had a Parisian pattern for her gown, for they were all the latest fashion, though widely varied in trimmings and individual style. Inside, they were greeted by the host and hostess, who introduced Mr. Frederick Butler, a dark, debonair man who exuded confidence and polish. He kissed her gloved hand.

Perhaps her excitement at hearing the orchestra showed in her eyes, or the light caught her hair in a particularly flattering way, but Mr. Butler immediately claimed her for two dances during the course of the evening.

The ballroom sparkled with light and throbbed with music and cheer, but Penny was obliged to sit out several dances while she awaited her promised partner, as she was married, and unmarried ladies seemed to be more desirable partners. Her foot tapped impatiently as she made boring conversation with other married women, who did not really accept her at all as one of them, and she knew it. In fact, she disliked them and they disliked her. She left, to speak to Miss Aldridge who was sitting alone, and returned a few minutes later, unseen by them. She heard them speak disparagingly.

"A laundress! Imagine."

"That class of people, when they are out, overdress in the most gaudy manner. Bright yellow for a married woman! She wants to be seen, to be noticed, a vulgar thing."

"She should have stayed at home with her husband. How must he feel, when his wife is out at a Ball, and he is completely helpless?"

But at least one voice defended her, so they were not all horrid.

"Don't be unkind, Helen. I'm sure her life is hard enough. I'm sure he wished her to have some amusement tonight."

"Beatrice, you're so charitable as to make me ill."

She seated herself quietly and they fell silent. When Mr. Butler came to claim her for his two dances, they stared. Though at least thirty-five, he was the most handsome man in the room.

He danced beautifully. Penny was not a good dancer, not having had any opportunity to learn, and she owned that to him.

"Really?" he said, astonished. "Why was your education so neglected?"

"It may surprise you to know," she said. "But everybody else knows, and so you might as well, I was a tradeswoman before my marriage, so I had not time to learn these fine things in life. Those women over there - "she jerked her head toward where she had been seated."- despise me for it."

"Oh, I shouldn't mind them. English manners are oppressive. A year in Paris or Venice would do them all a great deal of good. Allow me to lead, Mrs. Eglinton. Just follow, one, two three, one, two three, there, you're getting the hang of it already! No, they have nothing at all to recommend them, only a dullness after years of education in how to stifle natural feeling. Unlike you, I suspect, Mrs. Eglinton. You have a natural way about you that I find refreshing and different."

She did not really know what he meant.

When he made his bow, he asked for two more dances later, after supper, which she was glad to accept. But she wondered what her mother-in-law would think. Where was Mrs. Eglinton?

She decided to go in search of her. There were a few little rooms leading off the ballroom, and the doors were slightly ajar. She peered in the first one, it was empty. From the second one, she heard the sound of stifled sobbing. She drew nearer, very quietly. It was an ante-room decorated with palms and other tall plants, and she could not be seen, but in the dim light she saw three figures seated together. Mrs. Eglinton was weeping quietly, and Dr Aldridge and his sister were on either side of her, comforting her. Dr. Aldridge pressed her hand, perhaps a liberty he allowed himself because he was a doctor.

She withdrew. Poor woman! Was it Martin's condition that tore her heart, or her husband's coldness? For she had seen the latter. He showed her no affection whatsoever. How dreadful it must be to be married to somebody of such coldness!

After supper, at which Mrs. Eglinton appeared to be her normal self, Penny had two dances with a middle-aged gentleman, and two more with a morose partner whose name she did not know, and then Mr. Butler claimed her again. She hoped there would not be gossip and tried to look as if she was not enjoying his company quite as much as she was. He was telling her of his travels – to Vienna, Paris and other exotic places that she knew little about.

As they prepared to part, he said: "I hope to see you again, Mrs. Eglinton. I have much to tell you, of my trip to New York for instance, and I have been to St. Petersburg also – the most beautiful city – but we must part now. The violins are beginning the polka." He bowed.

They drove home. Mrs. Eglinton asked her how she enjoyed herself.

"I'd never attended a Ball before, but I was at ease as the evening went on." she said.

"That Mr. Butler you danced with – a charming man, but a bit of a bounder, I've heard people say."

"Oh, if I had known he had a reputation, I would not have stood up with him."

"It is all right, in a public place, and everybody understands your situation. Martin does not want you to be cooped up in the house. It is no harm for you to dance."

Penny wondered about the last comment. She was not convinced harm had not been done, for she remembered being close to her partner, his firm hand on her back, her hand on his shoulder, as they whirled about the floor. She knew now how to waltz properly, but he had said he wanted to teach her the polka and he dearly hoped to see her again.

It was a rather forward thing for him to say, and she hoped she would not meet him.

She went straight to bed, forgetting to say 'goodnight' to her husband. His mother was more kind, she went in to his room and told him that it had been a very, very dull evening. She said that Penny had gone to bed with a bad headache, as she did not want him to know that she had forgotten to come and see him. This marriage was largely her doing, she thought, and she'd never be critical of Penny unless she was really unkind, and she was not – she was young and thoughtless. She had no doubt that Penny loved Martin, or was rapidly coming to that point.

CHAPTER THIRTY-TWO

Penny remembered the next morning that she was supposed to have bid goodnight to Martin and she felt guilty. She could hear Benjamin getting him up so she had to wait until he left the room before she went in to speak with him.

"How is your head?" he asked as soon as he saw her. "Mother told me."

How crafty of Mrs. Eglinton!

"It's much better."

"You must tell me all. Who did you dance with?"

He listened, and if when she mentioned Mr. Butler's name, and her colour changed at all, or her tone of voice changed, he didn't mention it.

"He's a wild one," he said. "Stay away from him. Some of these men out in the colonies come home rather reckless. He made a fortune in Madras, to add to the riches he inherited from an uncle."

"I've every intention of staying away from him," she replied with indignation. "I'm not going out again, and he won't come 'ere."

But Mr. Butler called to the Eglintons that very day, and the young Mrs. Eglinton was obliged to sit a half-hour in his company. She kept her eyes down.

Penny was in the habit of taking an afternoon walk with her mother-in-law. However, one day soon after she went alone, as Mrs. Eglinton had a cold. Penny went along Clifton Walk as far as the turn for Clifton Drive, then crossed the street to a quiet wooded area, laced with pathways, known as Eyre Park. It was a golden October day, and leaves were falling gently about her. She walked along the path, nodding to the nurse who walked a baby out, stopped to warn some young lads that if they didn't stop larking around in a tree they'd fall and break their heads; then, around a corner, she came face to face with Mr. Butler. He looked not so much surprised as pleased, doffed his hat and bowed. They had a few minutes conversation about the weather and the leaves, and then he asked if she would mind if he accompanied her on her walk.

What harm was it, she reasoned. But she declined to take his arm when he offered it.

He began to speak of his travels. He did not mind telling her that he had a great deal of money, and now intended spending much of his time in Switzerland, which he described to her as sparkling like a diamond in its beauty.

Before they parted, after a half-hour, he asked her if she often walked there, and Penny was alert enough to reply:

"I think you know that I do, for when you visited our house the other day, did you not bring the subject around to the many fine walks you had heard were in the neighbourhood, and didn't Mrs. Eglinton say that we often walked in Eyre Park?"

He smiled. "Am I so transparent, then?"

"No, but you are very clever I think."

"I hope you do not cease to walk here then, in this Park."

Oh, here was the devil tempting her again! She could tell him, quite bluntly, that what he was hinting at was wrong, but she did battle with herself.

It wouldn't be any harm to meet a friend now and then in a public place, she thought. For they had met neighbours who she had openly greeted, as she was not doing anything wrong at all in his company. So she smiled, and her smile was her consent. Mrs. Eglinton did not like to walk every day.

Hurrying home, she felt pangs of guilt. She was a married woman. But Martin would not begrudge her friendship with another man, when it was all open and public. On the other hand, she was not about to tell him about it. She met Mr. Butler the following day, and the day after that. Anytime Mrs.Eglinton was with her, he did not appear, but there were many times she was too busy to attend her, and Mr. Butler crossed her path. She was happy to see him.

She played cards and chess with Martin, but her heart was faraway. He noticed, worried.

CHAPTER THIRTY-THREE

I t was shortly before Christmas; Martin pulled himself up from the bed and sat on the side. His arms had become uncommonly strong now. Would that his legs would follow! He placed his wrists on the free-standing frame that the carpenter had built and heaved himself to an upright position. Perhaps, this time, when his feet met the ground, he would feel something. Perhaps they would wake up and begin to work again. Perhaps, perhaps, perhaps! But no – he fell back upon his bed.

A new doctor had been summoned to see him at his father's behest. He had attended him in November. His name was Sowerberry and he had come all the way from Edinburgh. He had refused to allow Dr. Aldridge to be present at his examination, and also refused to allow him to give a History of the patient he was about to see. He also refused to state his specialty. He never gave a report either to Dr. Aldridge or to Martin's wife or mother before he left, saying he would make his report to Martin's father, who had engaged him, would not stay for any refreshment, and quit the house.

Dr. Sowerberry had been a sullen, quirky kind of fellow and Martin had not taken to him in the least. He'd asked him a great deal of questions, many of a personal nature, which Martin had forebore to discuss. He asked him to describe his dreams and suggested that he suffered from nightmares and hallucinations, when Martin had said nothing of the sort. Martin was very happy to see the back of him, and hoped never to see him again. Dr. Sowerberry did not seem at all interested in discussing whether he would ever walk again. As soon as he left, he put him out of his mind, as he had other things to worry about.

He had been married only six months, and he could see that Penny was often elsewhere in her mind, if not her heart. He was horribly conscious that he had asked too much, far too much of her, in marriage. She, born in poverty and deprivation, working her fingers to the bone scrubbing clothes, had seen a future of ease and plenty, and had not hesitated. But he had hoped that she liked him too, and that together they would try to conquer this impediment to their happiness.

No intimacy, no children.

Now there were rumours about her, for the servants were talking, and Benjamin had heard something in the Servants Hall that he felt he ought to know. A nanny out walking had seen her several times in the company of Mr. Butler. It may be innocent, but the neighbours were of the opinion that young Mrs. Eglinton was being unfaithful to her husband. He was sure it had not gone that far.

"Penny," he said gently to her when she came in to kiss him goodnight, "Stay a little while. I want to talk with you."

She sat on the side of the bed. The fire was still burning in a warm glow, and his bedside candle showed his concerned, serious countenance. He took her hand.

"Remember when I said that Love would come, Penny. Is there any sign of it?"

She looked down. He pressed her hand again and again.

"Are you happy with me, Penny? Tell me, be honest. Is the sacrifice too much?"

She took her hand away from his quickly, and covered her face.

"I can't pretend any longer, Martin. I don't want to hurt you! I wish I hadn't misled myself into thinking that fine things alone would make me happy! Please don't be hurt by what I say!" She threw her head on his chest, and he stroked her hair. "You said that love would grow – and I do love you more every day. You're good, and kind, a far better person than me. But I wish we – I don't know –about our future, Martin, I'm sorry. I am very sorry!"

He continued to stroke her hair, tears running down his cheeks. These dastardly legs! He became more determined than ever to conquer whatever it was within him that was stopping him from walking. He'd go to every doctor in England. He'd go abroad. He'd go as far as Russia, America, anywhere!

They lay like that for a long time. She clung to him. They kissed and caressed each other, and what happened next was natural for any other couple, but for them, it was a triumph. They were able to come together as husband and wife. They felt very, very happy, and fell asleep in each other's arms with a happiness and a new closeness to each other.

CHAPTER THIRTY-FOUR

Penny returned to her room the following morning before the maids were up. How funny it was that she and Martin were acting as if they were secret lovers! It should be the most natural thing in the world to wake up together. Their secret was theirs alone, for now. It would take a little more planning before they could arrange their room so as to spend all their hours together.

She loved Martin! Mr. Butler – what was he? Only a vain cad. An oily, ageing cad! She would never go to Eyre Park again. Never! Martin was tender, loving and made her feel safe and cherished. She could cope with Martin's being crippled, if they could lie together at night and she could have his children. What joy they would bring to the home! He would be a great father, too, wise and kind, unlike his own.

She crept to his room nightly, awoke in his arms, and they kissed before they parted as if they were never to see each other again, though it would be a separation of only a few hours.

One night, Martin confided to her everything that had happened in Peru. He bared his heart and soul. It poured out of his heart like molten lead. She listened, horrified. After he had finished, he took a deep, deep breath.

"Did you mind, that I told you all of that horrible business?"

"No, Martin, I'm happy you did. You have not uttered a word to anybody about what happened?"

"No, never. I trust you, Penny. My wife and my best friend."

In the following few days, Martin mentioned that he felt a load had lifted from him. He felt bright and optimistic about their future.

"It's as if I was being pursued by a wild beast in the jungle hidden by trees; constantly threatening to pounce, to come upon my neck and deliver a fatal wound. Speaking of this, this beast, has robbed it of its power. Is it not very odd, Penny?"

"I'm sure I don't understand it at all, but if you feel better, that's good news!"

When Martin woke up the following morning, he felt a brief, warm sensation in his toes. Very fleeting, but the first thing to give him hope since he had been stricken.

CHAPTER THIRTY-FIVE

A letter was brought to Penny. She did not recognise the writing, but thought it was a male hand, so she managed to hide it from Mrs. Eglinton. Alone later, it was as she suspected - a letter from Mr. Butler, plaintive in tone. He complained that he had waited for her at Eyre Park every day, and she had not come. Was she ill? He hoped not, for he could not bear to hear that she was ill and that he would be unable to visit her. He wrote in a rambling style, perhaps in an effort to interest her anew in what had interested her before, of his travels in various parts of the world. He ended by saying:

You might think me a very happy man, because I am successful. But in Love, alas, I am unlucky and wonder if I am always destined to be so. There has not been one time when I looked upon some wonder, some still blue lake or high snowy mountain, that I felt deeply the lack of a beloved to share it with. I would love our two hearts to throb as one when we behold the Bridge of Sighs, or the beautiful sunset behind Lake Como. Will you come with me, Penelope? I cannot be complete without you. I am off to London soon; come to me at 12 Park Street in Mayfair.

She threw the letter into the fire and watched it burn to ashes.

"That's the end of you, Butler," she said to herself. "How could I have been so foolish?"

CHAPTER THIRTY-SIX

Late in January, Mrs. Eglinton opened a large packet of letters at breakfast. Taking one out and beginning to read, she gave a faint exclamation of horror, before falling helplessly back upon her chair, as if she had suddenly lost the use of all faculties.

"What is it, Mrs. Eglinton?" Asked Penny, anxiously. She reached for the letter. But her mother-in-law put out her hand. "Don't." she whispered. She took the letter, re-read it, folded it and left the table. Penny heard her go upstairs, taking the packet with her.

Mrs. Eglinton retired to her room for a time. After Martin was up and downstairs, she went to the drawing room, and shut the door.

This would not do! She was his wife, and if it concerned him, it concerned her also!

"It was that quack Sowerberry. That was his intent all along! Oh Mother, have I any rights at all in the matter? This is too horrible!" She heard as she pushed open the door.

Mother and son looked stricken with distress.

"I will tell her, Mamma. Alone." Martin indicated that his mother should leave.

"I am sending for Dr. Aldridge directly," she said, as she rushed away.

"Be seated, Penny. I have something quite awful to tell you. It's truly dreadful. Do you remember that doctor who came to see me of late? Dr. Sowerberry from Edinburgh?"

She nodded.

"He made a report to my father - that I am not of sound mind." His voice dropped in horror and shame, before it rose anew in great emotion. "My father has planned this, he engaged him for that very purpose, to have me declared insane, and incapable of making my own decisions. And he said that I was insane at the time of – at the time of – "

"Not our marriage!"

"Our marriage. My father is still in England, he is in London, stayed here for this very purpose, no doubt - and he has had our marriage annulled. A quick and easy matter, as I was *incompetent to take vows*." He quoted from the letter.

"Dr. Sowerberry had not seen you at the time of our marriage!" she protested.

Martin shook his head, and there was a desperation in his movement. "It does not make a difference. My father has not only got the opinion of this Dr. Sowerberry, but Sowerberry has also consulted with Dr. Graves, who came to see me last year, and he has prevailed upon this Dr. Graves to be in agreement with him."

"But we are married! We are!"

"All is lost, Penny." He said quietly, "Here is the letter. It is from my father, and encloses the report made by the doctors, and the certificate of annulment. He makes it clear enough. I have no rights now. I have no control over money, where I go, what I do, who I see, it is all given to my father. He is my guardian, as if I were a child again. I have lost everything. Worst of all, I lose you."

Martin buried his face in his hands.

"I will never forgive him this," he said through his teeth. "Other things I can, perhaps, but not this!"

"If the marriage is annulled, what does that make me?" she whispered.

CHAPTER THIRTY-SEVEN

Miss Anne Aldridge arrived. The doctor was out on a call, but she had left a message that when he returned home, he was to proceed to Eglintons directly. Mrs. Eglinton had also sent for Matilda, who arrived with her baby boy and the nurse. Dr. Aldridge arrived in the late morning and the conference of shocked, distressed people took place over a hastily cobbled-together lunch of soup, cold meats, cheese and bread.

"I'm shocked beyond belief," the doctor exclaimed, when it was all explained to him. "It is a preposterous diagnosis; there is no basis for it. We all know Martin is in his right mind."

"I can understand how, perhaps, my father searched and found a doctor who would agree to a diagnosis he had decided upon, but for Dr. Graves to concur – that I cannot fathom."

"It's possible that Sowerberry knows Graves, and perhaps has something against him – perhaps an indiscretion, or an error, which if known could ruin him. This is unprofessional and unconscionable!"

"The very worst aspect is that my marriage to my beloved wife has been annulled," said Martin, in a very angry, hurt tone.

Penny had been speechless almost the entire morning. To have found Martin in her heart, and now to lose him had made her almost mute with grief. Added to that was the injustice of this, the outrage, the fear that his father could still hurt him in more ways, having rendered him almost helpless.

"There must be a way to fight this," she said in a low, dejected tone.

"Yes, there must!" said Mrs. Eglinton, "But I am quite in despair about it."

Penny noticed that neither Dr. Aldridge nor his sister gave any regard to herself. Her heart felt heavy in her breast. They had heard the rumours, then. And thought Martin well rid of her. Perhaps they thought it better she depart, and then the 'insanity' diagnosis might be lifted, or forgotten.

"Father cannot mean to do so much harm." Matilda said. "You are still Martin's doctor, Michael. And what you have done for him so far is helping him greatly."

"My leg muscles are still present to a large degree," Martin said. "I can feel sometimes, a warmth and tingling in the toes. I may yet walk!"

"Oh, Michael," said Anne suddenly. "I brought your post with me, in case you have to go on another call directly after lunch." She reached for her reticule and brought out several envelopes. He leafed through them.

Mrs. Eglinton saw the handwriting on one, and heaved a sigh.

"Please open that one, as I am in fear of it." she said, handing him an unused knife. They waited. Martin too had recognised the writing as that of his father's.

"I am dismissed from this family's care," he said to the company.

CHAPTER THIRTY-EIGHT

"You must leave the house before he comes," Mrs. Eglinton told her nervously. "I cannot answer for what will happen when he walks in the front door and finds you still here. You should have taken that offer he made you, Penny!" she added in a despairing voice. "If you had, it would have been better!"

"He is such an evil man!" Penny burst out. "But where will I go? What will I do?"

"You can go home to your mother, surely?"

"Did Mr. Eglinton make any provision for me at all?"

"Not a penny. He demands that any jewellery that belonged to our family be handed back, and you may keep everything else."

Penny's mind was busy. She had her gowns and her jewellery and shoes and all the other items. Suddenly, they meant little to her, if she could not have her beloved Martin.

She would have to live at home for a time, until she decided what to do.

"My husband said that should you ever return here, or try to contact any member of this family, that he will send Martin to an asylum. For his sake, never come back, Penny!" Mrs. Eglinton gripped her arm. "I am the architect of this terrible mistake. How I wish I had never thought of this marriage! Go, please, I don't want to see you anymore!"

To be so horribly rejected! Her heart was suddenly flooded with longing to see her mother and grandmother. It would be such a solace to hear their familiar voices.

"I must go now, Martin," said Penny, wrapped in her cloak and ready to leave, her eyes red from crying. "I will never forget you."

"Oh, Penny, if we could but run away together! What will you do? You could teach reading, or become a companion – you have education and manners enough to get a situation."

"Your mother has given me a reference, saying I was companion and assistant to her. It will be a help. Don't worry about me, Martin. Don't forget your exercises, and your elixirs."

"Don't forget to pick up your aitches," he said, managing a wan smile. It had been a source of amusement to them. "I have been hearing more and more of them, and that's a good thing!"

"Yes, loving Husband," she said, emphasising the H. "For you always will be that in my Heart."

"Penny, I must entreat you to do something."

"What is it? I will do anything for you."

"You must forget me. Make a new life. You are free, completely free, in the Law."

Penny lowered her head. She felt too moved to speak.

Mrs. Eglinton appeared in the doorway, anxious.

"Are you ready, Penny? The carriage is here."

Penny and Martin shared one last kiss, and she left him.

CHAPTER THIRTY-NINE

Her mother and grandmother were stricken with dismay when she arrived, trunk and all, in a carriage to their door. The trunk was lifted in and it seemed to fill the living-room. She sat down and related all in front of a small, feeble fire.

"And I do love him now," she declared, with a little look of reproach towards her mother. "I love him and what is more, we have been man and wife, and that's what makes this situation more shameful for me, and I'm completely innocent in the situation! We love each other, and we must separate!"

"That old Mr. Eglinton deserves hangin' for 'e 'as as good as murdered 'is son. What if 'e sends 'im to an asylum?"

"That's why I can't ever go back," she said sadly.

"So what are you going to do, Penny? You can 'ave your little room back, but you'll 'ave to find a job pretty quick. And we 'ave bad news too; I've been turned off from the Mill for the winter. The demand for cotton is low just now, the Masters say, tho' I'm not sure I believe them. We owe rent for six weeks now, and 'ave pawned everything."

"Oh, Mamma! I'm sorry to hear that. Why did you not tell me? Are you still angry with me, and proud? I will get a situation as soon as I can. And I have a little money, you and Grandmamma need a better fire, for one thing, I will see to it without delay. And, we can pawn some of my dresses and other things."

CHAPTER FORTY

P enny read the advertisements in the newspaper daily. She saw nothing to suit her. So very early in the New Year she wrote one: *Useful Companion, age 19, seeks position. She is a good reader, is industrious with her needle, respectable and steady, and might suit a home with an invalid. References.*

Three replies came promptly. One was from a man in Deansgate, seeking a companion for his aunt, who was in need of 'much nursing.' The second was from Lever Hill, from a woman who wanted a companion who would also be her housekeeper; the third was from a family with an elderly woman from Leeds who though lively of mind, was going blind and needed help with her daily activities, had heretofore been fond of reading, but now needed the services of a reader and companion. This looked to be the most promising and she answered it, and within a few days had boarded a train for Leeds.

She felt a little nervous, but she remembered how Mrs. Eglinton told her about her 'demeanour' and how well she had conducted herself in society when a member of the

Eglinton household. All her learning came to her rescue as she faced her prospective employer Mr. Wells. He was a rather shy little man, but learned, as she knew from his library, and she answered his questions with confidence. She remembered her 'aitches', and was taken to see the elderly woman and was asked to read a Shakespeare sonnet to her.

"She has a pleasant voice," said the old woman. "But did you tell her, Percy, that we are to move to London?"

"I was coming to that, Mother." He said in haste, "We are to move within three weeks. If you accept the situation, it will be understood that you will come with us, to a very nice area, by the way, Chiswick. Mother wanted a Northern girl to attend her, so when I saw your advertisement, I thought we would be lucky. Though I am sure there is nothing wrong with London girls."

"I like the Northern accents much better," said Mrs. Wells. "Do you want to think it over, Miss Fowler?"

Everything was in her favour here except the move to London, but perhaps it would be better for her to leave Manchester. She had often thought so in the last two weeks. There were so many reminders of her sorrow. She thought of Martin constantly, cried every night, and wrote him letters that she never, of course, posted. Betty was still in the employ of the Eglintons, and brought her tidbits of news, which caused her pain. Mr. Eglinton had returned home. He and Mrs. Eglinton had had a great argument. Mr. Eglinton thought she had been unfaithful! With Dr. Aldridge. But how was Martin? Betty had no news of him.

Penny accepted the position and began work the very next day. She left almost all of her money with her mother, who made no objection this time. She hesitated greatly to part with her gowns, the better ones. Might she not need them in

London? She kept two carriage dresses, two walking dresses, three morning dresses, three evening gowns, hats, shawls, reticules and many accessories to match. All she took with her she had come now to consider as necessary to her life. The ballgown, lesser gowns and shawls, and the remaining jewellery she gave her mother to makeover or to sell. She calculated that it would be enough for at least three months, at which time she would send them more money, and regularly after that.

CHAPTER FORTY-ONE

Martin pulled himself up in bed and pushed his legs out, as he did every morning. He'd dreamed, as he did often, that he was walking. He'd woken up and found that there was now sensation in one foot. He'd rubbed it and for the first time since his illness, it was not like rubbing a stick. He felt it!

Benjamin had left. Until he found another man to help him, Martin had to use sheer determination to help himself, with the help of the footman, who was too busy to be able to help him very much. He soon found that not having somebody to help him was making him do more.

"I have to try harder, to walk. Then I can get this ridiculous diagnosis done away with. I have to find doctors who will reverse this nonsensical state of things. I knew what I was doing when I made vows to Penny. I want her to come back. I must walk again."

He gripped the frame with his wrists and hauled himself to a standing position, and to his delight felt the backs of his knees against the bed frame. He wobbled a little, put more weight on his wrists, and held it before he fell back, as he did every morning.

Only this time, he had also felt the rough threads of the mat against the soles of his feet. His heart soared, and determined to try again. His feet answered again, firmer this time. He tried to lift one, but it was too much to ask, and he fell backwards again. But there was progress!

CHAPTER FORTY-TWO

Penny was overawed by London. Tall stately houses, fine carriages, handsome teams of horses, and the smart fashions of the London women made her feel old-fashioned.

The interior of the Wells townhouse was grander than Eglintons. But she was not a family member here; she was an upper servant. She had her own room, small, with a view of chimneys and rooftops. The wardrobe was too small for her gowns. They'd been surprised that her trunk had been so large, and she'd had to say that she was the same size as her last mistress and had been given many of her clothes. She was to be paid quarterly but it was too long to wait until Lady Day on 25th March, so she had to ask for an advance.

Her days were easy. She helped Mrs. Wells' maid to dress her and do her hair, read to her after breakfast, read her post and wrote replies dictated by her, and in the afternoon, when Mrs. Wells napped, she was free for a few hours. She went out and explored Chiswick but her heart was not in anything. She was heartbroken, but had to hide her moods, for she had told them that she was cheerful, in the interview.

One day when out walking toward Chiswick House, a noted landmark, she heard her name called, only it was not "Miss Fowler", it was *'Mrs. Eglinton.'* She turned around and blushed a little to see a familiar face, that of Mr. Frederick Butler.

"When I turned that corner," he began, "I thought I was dreaming. For there was my Love, my own Penelope, here in the Metropolis! Have you come to see me? No? I am so disappointed! You are glad to see me though, are you not? Say you are, even a little! You broke my heart, you little minx? What are you doing in Town? Shopping with your mother-in-law?"

"You must not call me Mrs. Eglinton any longer, Mr. Butler. My marriage to young Mr. Eglinton was annulled, very unfairly I believe, as does Mr. Eglinton, and I have left Manchester. I am Miss Fowler again."

"Annulled!" he made no further comment. "So what are you doing now?"

"I came to London as companion to a Mrs. Wells in Chiswick."

"It sounds very dull," he said. "You do remember where I live, I told you, you know, very particularly. I'm leaving for Switzerland in early summer, and plan to live there next winter. Will you come with me?"

Penny was surprised at the suddenness of the invitation and blushed. His meaning was obvious. She looked at the pavement.

"It would not be proper," she said.

"I should tell you," he said, "that I am not the marrying type."

"Since I have no intention of marrying," Penny said. "Unless it is to be remarried to Mr. Eglinton, and I'm not going to be your mistress, I'll decline your offer."

"What a disappointment! The very best carriages and inns; banquets and balls at which the crowned heads of Europe are seen! The lucky lady will be fitted out with silks and organdies for summer and minks for winter! If you do happen to change your mind, I'm at -?" he stopped, smiling, to see if she remembered. She did not.

"12 Park Street," he said. "You are a charming young woman, Penny. I do so like you very much. May I be of use to you on your present journey?" he offered his arm, but she declined.

"12 Park Street," he repeated, and touched the tip of her nose with his gloved finger, before he bowed and departed.

Penny sighed with relief, yet it was mixed with a little regret. She frowned at the thought of losing the splendid opportunity of seeing the world and travelling in style. Her occupation was already very predictable and boring, with no opportunity for making friends.

CHAPTER FORTY-THREE

Only one or two mornings later, Penny became ill while reading to Mrs. Wells and had to excuse herself. She lay down for a half-hour, and then felt perfectly well again. The following morning, it happened again, and the morning after that. By now, she was embarrassed. Why was she feeling ill every day, at the same time? On the fourth morning, Mrs. Wells was not at all pleased. She insisted on her seeing her own doctor, who came that afternoon.

He made his report to Mrs. Wells, who called Penny to her after he had left.

"Miss Fowler," she began in a severe voice. "No, do not sit. You must leave my employ without delay. I find myself outraged beyond belief! I thought you were an innocent girl of good character, but now I see all. I should have known, when I saw the quality of your gowns, and your fine bracelet, and the myriad other signs of pampering, that you were the mistress of some man who has now cast you off. You have deceived me! Did you think I'm a blind old fool, and would not discover your condition?"

"My condition?" cried Penny, with great distress.

"Yes, your condition! Whose mistress were you, foolish girl? You cannot stay here, you must pack your trunk directly and leave this house!"

Penny sank into a chair, in spite of Mrs. Wells' instruction to her to the contrary.

"My condition?" she repeated.

"Unless you are very ignorant, it can be no surprise to you that you are – *enceinte* – you are breeding." She said.

The family way! That explained the personal questions of the doctor, which she had, in all innocence, answered, and the humiliating examination. That the doctor did not tell her, but reported her condition to Mrs. Wells, was an outrage to her! She was thrown into a turmoil.

"But Mrs. Wells, you don't know the truth! I was married! I was! My marriage was annulled against my wishes -"

"No, do not lie to me! Ring the bell, you wicked girl!"

Numbed, Penny obeyed. The parlour maid was in the room within a few moments. Mrs. Wells told her to help Penny pack her trunk and instruct Vernon to call a cab to take Miss Fowler to wherever she wished to go in the city.

CHAPTER FORTY-FOUR

P enny did not know where to tell the cab to go, so she said "A cheap lodging house." Her distress was deep as she sank back on her seat, and pondered this unimaginable crisis.

She was having Martin's baby, which was a joy, despite everything. But sorrow followed – she and the baby had no home, and no prospect of such. Should she make her way back to Manchester? What was left for her in Manchester?

The cab brought her to a modest lodging which was exorbitant, in her mind, in its cost, but this was London. Her trunk was brought up and all that evening, after a light supper, she pondered her situation.

There was no point in writing to Martin. His father would make good on the threat to send him away.

She saw one solution, and swayed back and fro with it all that evening. It would involve a great deception, but she was desperate. She could not be more than two months and she was not showing. The more she thought of it, the more determined she became that it was the only sensible course open to her. It was the only chance for her and for her child, to give herself into the power of Frederick Butler.

She would go there tomorrow and hope that he had not taken her rejection seriously, and would welcome her.

She dressed in her best gown and fur-lined cloak, purchased two jaunty ostrich feathers for her hat, chose her white kid gloves with the pearl buttons, and set off.

His house was very grand, standing three storeys high, with attic rooms. She rang the bell and pretended to herself that she was of noble birth, paying a call to an inferior. *Demeanour.*

The butler looked her up and down, and when she said she wished to see Mr. Butler, ushered into the upstairs drawing room. She took in her opulent surroundings. Flocked wallpaper of green and gold leaves. The curtains were gold velvet with gold and green valance. The matching seating felt luxurious, and the little oak tables, with their lampstands, shone. There were three mirrors and several large paintings. It took her breath away.

The door opened and Frederick came in.

"When Harkness announced a lady to see me, I hoped it would be you."

"I hope you can forgive my hastiness," Penny said, holding out her hand, hating herself but congratulating herself on her good acting. "When I began to think of you, and Switzerland, I began to long for both, and could not sleep until I had made up my mind to see you! I've been fighting myself, Frederick. But I've lost! Hopelessly lost, I'm afraid! I do hope you forgive me! I have not ceased to think of you since our meeting!"

He took her hand and kissed it.

"Is that the truth?" he asked. "You will come and live here, with me?"

"Yes, of course! I told you I couldn't stop thinking of you!"

"Nor I you," he repeated, his eyes holding hers.

He handed her over to Mrs. Perkins, the housekeeper, who led her to her rooms, a suite separate from Mr. Butler's. This was Aristocracy indeed! The bedchamber and dressing room was enchanting, blue and white with velvet pile carpet underfoot. Mrs. Perkins threw open the large wardrobe.

"Perhaps you will find something there that will fit you," she said. "They belonged to Mr. Butler's sisters. You will be expected to dress with elegance, for Mr. Butler likes to go out to dine and be entertained by his friends, and in his turn, entertain here."

"I have my own gowns." Penny told her. Mrs. Perkins raised an eyebrow.

"They might pass in Manchester," she said. "But not here."

Her own gowns were not at all as elegant as those in her room which had belonged to Frederick's 'sisters.' She had her doubts about them, and wondered if there had been other women before her.

"I'm afraid Perkins does not think my Manchester fashion will pass muster here," she said to Frederick over the most elegant table she had ever been seated at, with a tall candelabra gracing the middle. He was at one end, she the other, and there was room for several diners in between them, though this was not the dining room proper, which was almost the size of a ballroom. She did not see the sense of eating so far away from each other. Martin would have hated that too.

140

"You shall have new gowns," he said with generosity. "London fashion is far ahead of anything you saw before. You shall go to *Maison de Chantal*. Nobody can touch it for design and workmanship. I shall order the carriage for you first thing in the morning. Now as to tonight, you shall come to me after your bath."

Penny knew that this was, of course, inevitable, and a very important part of her plan. She had to act as if she loved him, as she believed he loved her. It would solve everything, except the ache in her heart for Martin.

Madame Celine de Chantal of *Maison de Chantal* considered herself an artist. She believed that if an artist signed a painting, why should she not also sign her creations? Every garment that left her *Maison* had a cleverly-embroidered initial at the back, inside the bodice. CdeC.

Madame also had swathes of fabric, for she was very particular about what she worked on and who supplied her materials. Penny sat at a table and chose her fabrics. Her favourite was a lilac cambric with a delicate puce print for a day-dress, with three lines of puce satin ribbon throughout its length, to give her height, Madame said, but craftily, for it promised to flatten her stomach. For her evening dress, white silk with Valenciennes lace for trimming and sleeves, and sage ribbons to highlight the scalloped flounces in the skirt. Penny's head swam with the choices!

She used the opportunity of having clothes made which would cleverly disguise her condition until it was feasible to reveal it. If Madame de Chantal and her assistants guessed her true situation, they did not refer to it, but upon her request, made her bodices fuller than necessary and skirts wider in the front.

CHAPTER FORTY-FIVE

The leaves began to bud on the trees in Mayfair, the birds began to sing, the daffodils appeared in the park. Penny enjoyed her sumptuous surroundings. She'd never known wealth like this! Her gowns were beautiful and Frederick engaged a lady's maid to come to Switzerland with them. Thoughts of Martin became less and less with the distractions of her opulent surroundings, even the house at Chiswick seemed stifling compared to Park Street. She was a lady in an elegant area of London. Everything she saw, touched and used was of the best quality. Mrs. Perkins told her that her bedchamber and dressing-room were decorated in true 17th century French. Chinese satin brocade and the softest velvets made up the curtains in all the rooms. The back garden was heavenly as the weather warmed. She ordered her afternoon tea to be served there on the Italian marble table under the cherry blossoms.

As Frederick and his house became more important to her, she began to believe more and more that she would become his wife. Manchester was almost forgotten; the thought of writing to her mother on the best bond paper made her hesitate; or perhaps it was guilt that stilled her pen. Frederick was good-humoured, if selfish. She had no doubt of his being very selfish, and of being very out of humour when crossed. She thought that the servants looked down upon her. That would alter, Penny thought, when she became Mrs. Butler.

Perhaps she hadn't loved Martin much after all, she thought, as she drew her hand across the white damask tablecloth in the dining room which had gold and silver threads running through it. She wouldn't like to be the laundress in this house! She'd be terrified of damaging such valuable linens. But all those days were behind her…

She managed to conceal her condition from Frederick. He liked to go out in the morning in his gig, but she was not to go with him, or to be seen in daylight with him, which suited her perfectly at least until her time of sickness had passed. She sat quietly in a cosy parlour and pored over *The Ladies Monthly Magazine* to examine the latest styles.

Would she wait until they reached Switzerland to reveal her expectations? No, for she was beginning to show. April was almost out; he was making preparations – she had better tell him.

"I have a little news," she said, directly after dinner the following evening, as they drank coffee after the servants had left the room. She now loved coffee. "I hope you'll be happy, Frederick."

"Oh, what is it?" he asked. "Did you accept an invitation for us both to go to the de Brun's house party? I saw you talking with Mrs. De Brun the other night. You did not accept, I hope, without consulting me?"

"Oh no, nothing like that." Her heart beat fast. "It's about us. We're going to be joined by a little stranger."

He stared hard at her. "Whatever do you mean?"

Her heart began to hammer.

"I mean, we're going to become parents."

He got up and strode to the window, and cursed.

"You cannot be serious!" he said, hotly. Penny felt a sudden chill.

"I am serious."

Frederick cursed again, took up a candlestick and threw it at the china cabinet, where it smashed the glass.

"Frederick!" she cried, getting up from her chair immediately, distressed.

"What – why? This is ridiculous!" he said. "I don't want marriage, I don't want a family! Oh, why was I so foolish?"

"What do you mean?"

"You fool, Penelope! I hope you don't think I will be trapped into marriage."

"Trapped!" the statement had more truth than even he knew. "You said you loved me!"

"Yes, I do, but I don't love *it*. Get rid of it."

"I most certainly will not! How dare you suggest such a thing!" she was going to add, *'about your own child'* but did not.

"I know a druggist. You will go there tomorrow."

"No!" she cried, stamping her foot. "How can you speak that way?"

"How would you know so soon?" he added with sudden suspicion. "You are not here even three months! You may be mistaken, you know."

"I am sure!" she said. "And – you have to do the right thing by me, Frederick."

He made no answer, but left the room. She heard him go out; she knew not where. She waited up for him, trying to read, but the words made no impression upon her.

He came in about eleven o'clock. She was on the upstairs landing, about to go to bed, when she heard his key in the door.

"Well, Penelope," he said, seeing her and coming up at a rapid stride. "I've been making enquiries in Chiswick. You are a very deceitful, wicked woman. I made you an offer most women would accept with alacrity, and you rejected me. Then you come to me smiling, full of flattery, pretending you're in love with me! I did wonder at the alteration, you know.

"You're an actress," he went on. "You tried to use me. Martin Eglinton was not quite as helpless as people thought, was he? You're carrying his brat, and you tried to make me believe it's mine! What treachery, what wickedness! Eglinton's well shut of you and so am I! Leave this house! This moment!"

"No, no!" Penny was trying to take in all he said, it seemed too much, and as she tried to gather her thoughts together, tried to clutch at an excuse, an explanation, he grabbed her by the shoulders. "Frederick, please listen –"

"Did you not hear me? *I said*, leave this house. Immediately!"

"Immediately?" she said, numbly, beginning to accept his total rejection. "At this time of night?"

"Yes. How many times do I have to repeat myself, you witch?"

"I have to pack! Will you not have mercy, Frederick, and let me stay until morning?"

In answer, he pushed her toward the staircase and forced her down the steps.

"Let me get my belongings!" she cried, struggling.

"They're your keep!" he said. "Your food, wine, bed and board!"

"I paid for my keep!" she retorted, only to be pushed down the last three steps. She fell, but picked herself up immediately.

"What shall I do? Where shall I go?" she asked with terror as he pushed her outside.

"I don't know, I don't care, to the devil, to the Thames." He said, and shut the door in her face.

CHAPTER FORTY-SIX

She banged on the door, until evidently becoming sick of it, he got his coachman up and the carriage came around the front. Frederick was not in it.

"I have orders to take you to Spitalfields, Miss. Get in."

"Where's that? What shall I do there?" It was an unfortunate question, and she heard him laugh. He did not have to be polite to her now. The coach stopped after some time.

"This is the end of the journey, Miss. You're to go into that house, ask for Mrs. Dooley, and say Mr. Butler sent you with a recommendation." He laughed again.

The carriage was gone; she was left in front of a bawdy house. She'd seen them in Red Bank. Grandmamma would purse her lips and shake her head if they passed one, even in the daytime, she'd rush her past. Of course that had made young Penny curious, and she would be told that only bad women went into a bawdy house.

What an insult from Frederick Butler! She turned and walked up the street, past couples in the shadows, past drunkards lying on the paths.

It was all gone.

A man called out to her; then followed her for a time, before he gave up. She was walking deeper and deeper into streets of poverty, wretchedness and filth. She did not know where to go or what to do. Finally she sat down on a doorstep, broke down and wept.

It was all gone! Everything!

"What's this noise?" a woman with a candle opened the door behind her. "It's after midnight. Go an' bawl somewhere else." – spying the voluminous gown, with lace and ribbons trimming – "Ooh, you're a lady! What 'appened you? Were you robbed?"

"Yes!"

"Where's your conveyance?"

"Gone home!"

"If you walk up tha' way, you might find a policeman."

A policeman. What good would a policeman be to her?

"Please listen," she said. "I was the mistress of a rich man, and he threw me out because I'm expecting."

"Well and why din't you say that to begin with? Go around the corner to Dover Street and knock on the door of number three. There are do-gooders there that 'elp women. The Society for Distressed Women. I thought you was a lady an' could go 'ome." The door slammed shut.

It was past midnight; she made her way around the corner and within five minutes was inside a house; it must be a clean house, for it had a faint smell of polish.

"I'm Mrs. O'Hara," said the friendly woman who admitted her. "There's a bed upstairs, clean sheets an' all. I put 'em on myself this mornin'. Would you like a drink of water? I'm sorry to say the Society don't allow gin, though I don't think that'd be your drink anyway, would it, love?

"It's a rule that newcomers are to be given a bath, but I don't think we need to worry about you, Miss, and 'tis too late anyways." She eyed her finery. "Be careful of everything in here, Miss. There's some of them that pinch things. Though among the crowd I have at the moment, there isn't anybody light-fingered." She opened a chest of drawers and rummaged, pulling out a nightgown.

"Here you are, Miss Fowler. Can you get undressed in the dark? Just lay your clothes on the chair."

A few of the women in the room stirred, but were too sleepy to notice the newcomer.

She drank a cup of water and sank down on the bed. It was a hard bed with a lumpy mattress. She felt too shocked and tired to think, and fell into sleep, waking up every so often feeling the lumps and bumps and hearing occasional coughs and snores from the other women in the room.

The following morning, she awoke to find a little group in their petticoats around her chair. One young woman had lifted her lilac gown out of its folds and they were admiring it.

"Excuse us, Ma'am, but none of us has seen anyfink that fine in 'ere before." said one.

"Nor the jewellery," said another, eyeing the bracelet on her wrist.

CHAPTER FORTY-SEVEN

"Why isn't she writin'?" asked Grandmamma. "Somethin' must have 'appened. I don't know where to get in touch wiv her, the letter we sent to her address in Chiswick came back, and nowt to say why she wasn't there. Emma? Are you all right, child?"

Mrs. Fowler was coughing badly as she tried to peel a potato at the table. Her mother got up stiffly from the chimney seat and poured her a cup of water.

"You 'ave to see a doctor. I 'ave a guinea for emergencies in the old teapot. I'll send young Matthews." She went to the far wall and banged on it. She did not walk well now and was very short of breath. Even the few steps needed to go next door was too much, and the bang on the wall was the signal for their neighbours that the two frail women next door needed something.

Mrs. Fowler tried to say something, but she had not found her voice. Mrs. Matthews came in and taking one look at Emma, said she'd send Jimmy for the doctor directly.

"But where's Penny? Why isn't she writin'?" fretted Mrs. Pyke. "I always 'eard London was a bad place. Why din't she stay in Lancashire? You had better go to bed, Emma, to await Dr. Norris."

"I think Penny might need to come 'ome," Mrs. Matthews said quietly, worried.

Dr. Norris came and diagnosed pneumonia in both lungs. He looked around the drab room and empty shelves, and knew that his prescription of chicken broth and tripe would not be possible. The woman was suffering from undernourishment, and had no resources, internally or externally, to fight this infection with. It was thus with many people now, since many factories had closed and others were on short time.

Soon after Penny had left for London, word had got about in the neighbourhood that the women had valuables. One day when they had both been out at a funeral, they had come back to find that everything Penny had left them was gone. They were as poor as they had ever been.

"I will return tomorrow," he promised. "She has a daughter, I understand? You should try to get in touch with her."

Mrs. Fowler became worse. She began to struggle for breath. The neighbour stayed with her, and was relieved by another neighbour, Mrs. Pratt, around midnight.

"Mamma, what will you do? Who will care for you?" Mrs. Fowler asked, agitated, several times over the next few hours.

"We'll find Penny," promised her mother. She patted her hand. "That's my dear Emma. Be at ease, child." She blinked back tears.

Emma tossed her head from side to side, opened her eyes, murmured 'Harry!' in a loving, yearning voice while seeming to stare over Mrs. Pratt's head, who later said it made her come out *'all of a shiver'.* Finally Mrs. Fowler lapsed into a slumber, and soon passed into that Heavenly abode where every tear would be wiped away.

CHAPTER FORTY-EIGHT

"Percy? My post is here, will you read it to me please? I opened the envelopes." Mrs. Wells handed her letters to her son.

"Of course, Mother. Let's see…hmmm…a request from a clergyman representing Chinese Mission Society, asks for a donation for Famine victims."

"Throw it in the fire."

"A card from Hargreaves Perfumerie, inviting you to their *Exhibition of Finest Perfumes*."

"I will go. Though I cannot see too well, there's nothing amiss with my nose."

"This third letter is from a Reverend Parry in Red Bank, Manchester."

"I don't know him. He wants money, I'm sure. The fire."

There was a pause.

"Mother, this is not a request for a donation. This concerns the young woman we brought with us from Manchester. Good gracious!"

"That hussy? What can he want? What is it?"

"I shall read it."

Dear Madam

I write on behalf of Mrs. Esther Pyke, an elderly woman who lives in the Red Bank area of Manchester. She it was who gave me this address, as the last known of her granddaughter, Penelope Fowler or Penelope Eglinton, to give her the name when she was married, and indeed may yet be entitled to use, but that is another matter which I shall address below.

Mrs. Pyke is most anxious to trace her granddaughter. She must impart to her the sad news of her mother's death on April 27th this year, from pneumonia.

I have another reason for the desirability of contacting Miss Fowler (or Mrs. Eglinton). Mrs. Pyke has applied for Relief, and as a member of the Board, I am obliged to find if there is any relative or friend to whom she may apply before we admit her to Crumpsall Union Workhouse. She worked hard all her life, a laundress by trade until rheumatism crippled her. The disappearance of her granddaughter is of great distress to her, and I would be obliged if you could, by any means in your power, give any intelligence of where she may be.

My reference to 'Mrs. Eglinton' above requires explanation. Miss Fowler married Mr. Martin Eglinton, of Clifton Walk, last year, in good faith. However, an annulment was obtained upon the application of a Third Party, an objector, against her will, and against the will of her husband. It was a very dubious matter; the annulment may be invalid, as I am in grave doubt that an annulment to marriage could be granted so speedily.

You may see from all I have written above that it is very urgent that we find Mrs. Eglinton.

I remain, your servant, Reverend James Parry.

"Mother, did she not tell you she had been married?"

"She mentioned it, but I thought she was lying of course."

"You should have looked into it, Mother, a bit more!"

"She called herself *Miss*, and she was in a disgraceful condition. How could I have allowed her to stay one more minute in this house?"

"We must try to find her! You were too hard on her, Mother!"

"Percy, don't be ridiculous."

CHAPTER FORTY-NINE

Mrs. Eglinton found out that Emma Fowler died, from Betty. She too bore a message from Mrs. Pyke imploring her for news of her granddaughter, if she had any to impart.

"I have no news. But I shall write the poor old woman a note. She served me well for twenty years, I will send her something, I'm sure she needs it."

"She's in the Infirmary at Crumpsall Workhouse, Madam. She's very poorly too."

"That's sad to hear. But how odd they have lost track of Penny!" Mrs. Eglinton mused in concern. Had something happened to Penny? How would they know?

"How is young Mr. Eglinton, Madam?"

"He is coming along well, thank you. He walks with a stick, about his room, and out into the landing, and thinks he will try the stairs soon."

"That's great news, Madam! And did Mr. Eglinton return last week as expected?"

"He did, and he's rather unwell, I'm afraid. Since his return he has hardly left his room. His leg troubles him greatly. He has a large ulcer, and nothing will help it. We're having a visitor today, a Miss Kent, who is a distant cousin. She's staying with Mrs. Valley and they will visit almost daily so that will, I hope, distract Mr. Eglinton, and Martin also." Mrs. Eglinton mused that they all needed Miss Kent. Their lives had become confined. She could barely leave the house, as her husband became suspicious if he called for her and she was not in. He was convinced that she was having an affair.

The bell rang from his room. Millie went upstairs to see what Mr. Eglinton needed now. He rang the bell several times a morning.

"I hope he improves his health, Madam. Well if there's nothing else, I'll go." Betty took her money, set next week's washing on her hip and left.

Mrs. Eglinton swept upstairs to her husband's room, to meet Millie coming out.

"What was it, Millie?

"Only his pillow needed to be fixed again under his head again." Millie replied. "And to hand him water and to ask if Mr. Carson was contacted about the strikers."

Mrs. Eglinton sighed and entered the room. The windows were wide open because of the odour from his leg. His face was shrunken, but his eyes looked fiery as he watched her as she walked across the room.

"That maid has to go," he began. "She's impertinent."

"That is the sixth time you rang the bell this morning, dear. She's falling behind with her own work."

"You are all against me. I know that. Carson has not been in touch, so he must be with the strikers. Does he think I'm a fool? He made a deal with them. He's going to offer them more money. My money!"

"Just try to rest, dear." Mrs. Eglinton patted the sheets around him and he sank back upon the pillows.

She watched him as his eyes closed. Dr Mansfield had told her that he was in the last stages of syphilis. He had paranoia and would go insane, if death from the infected leg was not to take him first. An amputation was the only way to save his leg, but he would not be strong enough to survive the operation.

His mill had temporarily closed, the ships were lying by, business was at a standstill, the laid-off workers angry and discontented. All of these matters affected his mental condition. He was convinced that he had been defrauded, swindled and conspired against. He saw enemies everywhere.

"Mansfield is a quack," he said then, opening his eyes. "He's keeping me deliberately ill, so as to collect more fees."

It was pointless to answer to the contrary. Before Mansfield, there had been Lowe, and before Lowe, there was Fenwick. All greedy quacks.

"You're all waiting for me to die!" he shouted then.

She left the room and shut the door. She leaned her back against it, bowed her head and shook both hands in front of her, as if trying to shake off the misery collected in the room, the misery that lingered on her long after she left it. He would die soon. He had never loved her; she had never known his tenderness. What a wasted life! She thought of Dr. Aldridge. Everything had been proper about their friendship, and she had not seen him now for months. She missed him.

Martin's door opened and he came out, leaning on two canes. Here was a sunbeam, the light of her life! At least she could thank her husband for her children. Martin was improving daily. He still followed Dr. Aldridge's regimen with rigour, and the more Martin used his legs, the more they woke up to serve him. He had been driving himself very hard, with one goal in mind – getting Penny back as his lawful wife, if she had not married somebody else. He did not know.

"Mother, is there any point in speaking to Father about changing my diagnosis?"

She shook her head.

"He does not make any sense anymore, Martin."

They had unspoken thoughts. When Mr. Eglinton died, the guardianship would pass to Mrs. Eglinton, and she would engage her own doctors.

"Are you going in to see him?" she asked hopefully.

"No, Mother, I am not." Martin's tone was terse. If only his mother knew how much he struggled with forgiving his father – he was like Jacob who wrestled all night long with the angel, and got no rest! The wrongs his father had done against him devoured him at times – and at other times, he thought of Jesus, His Saviour, who had said: *"Father, forgive them, they know not what they do."* He tried to immerse himself in those words.

He loved his father, and remembered happier times, when he was a little boy, sailing toy boats on the pond with him, and being thrown in the air, and caught in strong arms, laughing. He had been very little then, but he remembered when he had loved his Papa.

At times, he felt that if his father made the slightest gesture of sorrow to him, that he would forgive him immediately.

"You are not going downstairs without help," Mrs. Eglinton gasped as Martin advanced toward the staircase, throwing the canes down to the Hall below.

But he was, and though she begged to go ahead of him, he would not have it, in case he fell and crushed her. He made his way down all the way, gripping the banisters on either side.

The front door opened, and Mrs. Valley entered, bringing her guest with her. They watched in great delight as Martin gained the Hall.

"Oh Martin!" she cried. "This calls for celebrations! Now that you're progressing so well, and may do stairs, you must come and visit us at Valley Lodge. You have not been out of this house for years now. Say you will come! Next month perhaps? Alice is staying for two months!" She quickly picked up a cane and handed it to him.

Martin, holding the cane in his left hand, balanced himself to shake hands with his distant cousin. She was slim with striking green eyes. His eyes were radiant with happiness at his success, but he was not aware that he looked very handsome. Last year, Miss Kent had jilted her fiancé a month before the wedding, believing him not to love her the way she felt she deserved to be loved, when he had not come to see her because his grandmother had fallen and broken her leg. He was not grateful for her, that was Mr. Collins' trouble. Her eyes followed Martin as he made his way to the dining room. Here was a man, a crippled man, who would, she was sure, be extremely grateful to be loved, and pay her all the attention due to her.

Matilda proceeded upstairs to see her father, who would tell her disturbing things about all the rest of the family, all of it untrue. He was a tragic case.

Mrs. Eglinton escorted Alice to the dining room, wondering when she would get a chance to tell Martin about Penny's mother.

"Mother," whispered Matilda later, "You should not allow Father to have matches."

"He needs his pipe, and you know the way he lights it over and over, and puts it by…but I will take the matches away, and he can ring for them. I think Miss Kent likes our Martin, you know! She glanced at him a great deal during lunch."

"Mamma, no more matchmaking, please."

CHAPTER FIFTY

P enny rubbed the sudsy sheets between her hands. She was a laundress again, and that stain, whatever it was, wouldn't come out. It had been left too long to dry in.

"Aroo all right there, Penny?" asked Mrs. O'Hara, with cheer.

"I'm all right, but it should have been treated straight away," she grumbled.

The day was warm, the streets outside the walls were noisy. The Shelter comprised of two terraced houses put together, and the back garden held several clotheslines. Sheets that had been white many years ago, and were now various shades of grey, and patched and mended with pieces of other sheets, were almost motionless in the still air, along with petticoats, bloomers and dresses, among them the fine gown that Penny had been wearing when she came in. She had selected a worn brown dress from the Shelter chest, and a shawl that had seen better days. Putting these on, this morning, had pushed her down to a place in her mind that was filled with dejection.

She was poor again. Poorer than she had ever been in her life before. She'd lost everything. Her mother's words returned to her, *'Remember Job. He had everything, and it was all gone...'*

And her own impudent rejoinder: *'But he got it all back again, Mamma!'*

Would she? Would she ever be rich again? Would she ever even have enough?

"Come in for a cup of tea," said Mrs. O'Hara. "It's time we had a chat."

Penny dropped the sheet back into the tub. Let it soak a bit longer. Mrs. O'Hara probably intended to enquire why she was here; and Penny was surprised that after several days, she had not asked her already.

The cup of tea lasted an hour in the small front parlour. By then, Penny had poured her heart out, and Mrs. O'Hara – Bernice – had listened carefully.

"We know of that *blaggard*," she said. "He has a succession of girls going in and out of his house, and when he's finished with 'em he gets his coachman to drop 'em off outside Dicey Dooley's. You were right to call it a bawdy house. She'd have lent you money, and then you'd have to work for 'er and 'er husband, on the streets, and they'll make sure you'll never be able to pay off yer debt, and 'ave to keep workin'. It nearly happened to me when I first came over, but for the kindness of this Society."

"How did you come to be in London?"

"It was the Irish Famine – ye must've heard of it. My family and I lived on the estate of Lord Lucan in Ballinrobe, County Mayo. He racked us all with high rents, for our little cabins no bigger than this parlour here. We lived on potatoes, and the Blight came upon it in '47, and we starved. My two little girls died. My mother and father were next. All my brothers went to America, two died on the ship, of typhus. Lord Lucan threw us all off the land. My husband and I came over 'ere. We weren't welcome in many places. He got a job, but we'd nowhere to live, and were refused in many houses, and he got cholera and died. So I'm on my own. I came to this Shelter a broken-down ghost of a woman. I din't want to live. Everyday I woke up I wished I had died in my sleep. But God gave me the strength. I live to help others."

"That's a terrible story," said Penny with great feeling. "How, when you wanted to die, did you get by from day to day?"

"I got by from hour to hour, minute to minute sometimes. God was with me in the minute, in the hour, in the day."

"I don't understand God's ways sometimes, do you?"

"No. But d'ye know, it wasn't God caused the Famine. T'was greed that caused it. Every little grain we grew had to be sold to pay the rent. And they were takin' ships of grain out of Ireland while the people 'ad nothing to eat.

"Two year ago," she went on, as if wanting to brighten up, "I met a good man, a widower, his wife and child died in the Famine and 'e came over for work. We got married. He does odd jobs here."

"Mick?" Penny had seen the man fitting a new pane of glass to a window, where an angry husband had thrown a stone against it.

"Tha's 'im. Mick."

"My children wait for me in Heaven." She said then, a misty look in her eye. "But Penny, from what you've told me, a great wrong was done you by the Eglintons."

"Perhaps, but I married for money, for riches. I think I got what I deserved. But Martin didn't do any wrong. Then I went to Mr. Butler for even more riches, and tried to pass the child off as his…that was wrong too."

"But not so wrong that you were thrown out on the street with nothing. Thank God you din't go to Switzerland with him, because he'd 'ave turned you out there as well as 'ere, and can you speak a word of Swiss or whatever it is they speak over there? Is there no hope at all of going back to young Mr. Eglinton, he should know about his child. They have to make provision for you and the babe, Penny. Go back and try. But stay 'ere as long as you need."

"Thank you, Bernice." Penny went back to her wash-tub. Many questions came to her, and scrubbing clothes was a good time to think.

Frederick had been so in love with her until she had moved in. What kind of man was that? She'd heard of some men who enjoyed the chase, or who only chased the women who they thought would never really take them seriously. Frederick never loved her, though he said he had. It was all a sham to get what he wanted. Martin would never have taken on like that!

And why, she was ashamed to ask herself, were her own feelings toward Martin so shallow? Thoughts of him had faded while she'd basked in opulence at Frederick's.

She loved costly things; fine clothes, precious stones and opulent surroundings. These were her loves. The thought made her feel very dejected, for she knew that these were false idols, distracting her from what was good and true, and that while she had been with Frederick, she had not given poor people a thought, not once had she parted with a penny to a beggar.

Oh God, can I begin again?

CHAPTER FIFTY-ONE

Martin awoke to smell smoke. He heard his mother scream. His father was bellowing in his room.

He got out of bed as quickly as he could manage, took his canes and went to the landing. It was thick with smoke, and he could see the flickers of flames under his father's door which was just at the top of the staircase.

His mother and the servants had appeared like shadows in the billowing reddish-grey light, he counted them – all had awoken and were present!

Hearing the terrified shouts from his father, he lunged toward the door.

"Mr. Martin, come back!" cried Hynes.

"He's on the other side of the door, and cannot open it. Mother locks it at night. Hynes – get me a towel soaked in water – from my room or Mother's – hurry!"

Martin lunged again towards the door. It broke open. His father was lying on the floor, his hand up weakly, reaching for assistance. Stretching in to pull him out on the landing, Martin had to balance on his own weight for a moment or two. The canes fell. He pulled his father out and then fell in the doorway.

His mother, Millie and Sarah pulled him out. His canes had caught fire. Hynes returned with a wet towel.

Mr. Eglinton had slumped against the landing banister, choking. Everybody was coughing.

"We must get out!" his mother said, "Martin, Hynes will help you! I will help your father! Millie and Sarah, go on ahead, call for help!"

"You go ahead, Mother, Hynes and I will help Father," Martin ordered. "Hynes - help me up."

The flames were shooting out of the door of Mr. Eglinton's room, threatening to engulf all of them if they did not flee.

"I can hold on to the banister with one hand, and hold on to Father with the other, if you will take his other side, Hynes, as we go. Put the towel on his face." Martin gasped for breath, but with a strong arm pulled his father to his feet. He hardly noticed that his own face smarted with pain.

They began the journey down, the flames following, consuming the wooden banister and steps behind them, as if ravenous for destruction.

They heard crackling and crashing behind them. Mrs. Eglinton, who had not gone farther than the front door, saw with terror the fire sweep the length of the landing and send it crashing to the ground floor in explosions of flame and sparks.

"Hurry, oh God, help them!" she cried. "Hurry, boys, hurry!" She ran forward to help, supporting Martin as they left the staircase behind them and reached the safety of the front door, helped by Millie who had run back.

The neighbours were astir. Somebody had run to alert the fire engines.

"Nobody left inside," Martin managed to say as they were escorted to the driveway. They lay their burden on the grass. Mr. Eglinton was moaning and in great shock, with severe burns. A neighbour had filled a bucket of water – seeing that it was useless to throw it on the fire, he soaked his handkerchief in it and bathed the head and hands of the burned man.

From the lawn, the family watched the house burn. Many people were now on the scene. There was a cry of horror as sheets of flame shot into the sky and the roof crumbled, crackled loudly and fell into the shell of what once had been Eglinton House.

Martin became aware after a time of the painful burns on his face and his hands.

CHAPTER FIFTY-TWO

Mrs. Valley bustled to and fro. Her mother had escaped injury, but was in deep shock and lying in bed. Her father was in another bed in the same room. He was dying. Martin lay in a smaller room, his face and hands bandaged. Dr Mansfield had already visited twice that day, and he had engaged the best nurses in Manchester that he knew of.

Mr. Eglinton rambled on and on. The word 'Why?' escaped him all the time. He sounded like a child who was deeply bewildered by some puzzle he could not understand.

"Why?" in a raspy, deep voice, his throat dried and sore.

"Why what, Papa? Is it the fire? We don't know," said Matilda for the hundredth time that day, though it was suspected that he had obtained matches from somewhere, was lighting his pipe, and fell asleep.

"Why? Why did he save me? I thought, when I saw him the other side of the door, that I had died and was sent before God, and that He was sending me to damnation, and my thought was that I deserved it! But it was my son Martin, who I treated so vile – my son who saved me!"

His eyes were too dried to produce tears. But his countenance said all.

"I felt a great Love. I can't explain it." He went on. "I can't – understand. My crippled son saved me, at risk to his own life, when I deserved to have died."

Matilda could not speak.

"I wasted my entire life. Money, what good is it? I had no time for people, no value for love, and if you only knew how I injured my son Martin – it was my fault he became ill!"

"Papa, papa!" This in a soothing voice. Matilda cast her eyes towards her mother's bed. She was awake and listening intently.

"Yes, my fault. Ask him to tell you the truth about Peru. I will get what I deserve from God."

His wife spoke.

"You think God is like you, do you? And that His mercy isn't enough to take away your sins if you repent them? What a proud, headstrong man you are. Matilda, read to him the Parable of the Prodigal son."

"I will see Martin. Where is he? I want to see him. I want to beg his forgiveness!" Mr. Eglinton struggled to get out of bed, but he was unable. Eventually Martin was persuaded to come in, and his father wept at the sight of his bandaged head and hands, as he reached out to touch them.

"Will you forgive me, son?"

"I forgive you, Papa." Martin said, and as he did so, he experienced a weight the size of a boulder roll away from his heart, and his anger melted into nothing. He sat with his father for quite some time. Mr. Eglinton was like a child now.

He died the following morning.

CHAPTER FIFTY-THREE

The knock on the door woke the house at 2am. Penny heard Bernice get up from her own tiny room next to where the women slept, and it was evident she was looking out the window as she shouted: "Who is it?"

"It's Tess, Mrs. O'Hara. Tess Barton! Let me in!"

"You again, Tess Barton." Penny heard Mrs. O'Hara say in a resigned tone.

"Ah don't take on, I've no money for a lodgin', and the Day Ward is too far for me to walk. Will you let me in for a few nights?"

"Are you in liquor?" shouted Bernice.

By now the entire house was awake.

"No, I am not. No' a drop has touched my lips."

"Yes she is," muttered one woman named Maria. "She's never any other way."

"Bernice should turn 'er away," said another.

"She won't do tha; she's afeard she'll come to 'arm on the streets. She's too soft, is Bernice."

"Watch yer valuables, anybody who has any," said Maria again. "She's a magnet for other peoples' goods."

"What valuables?" asked Julia merrily. "She's welcome to my comb that's only got three teeth left."

"Or my 'andkerchief what's been mended more times than I've 'ad hot dinners," said another.

"It's too late for a bath tonight, but first thing in the morning, d'ye hear?" scolded Bernice, as the door to the dormitory opened and she led the way ahead of a young woman with a bold countenance. Her face had once been pretty, but it had a worn look and was scarred.

Nobody greeted Tess, but watched as she made her way to an empty bed and flung her bundle on top of it.

"What you all starin' at?" she snapped at them. Then turning her eyes to Penny, she said. "Eh, you're new. I haven't seen you 'ere before. I 'eard there was a Lady in 'ere."

"I've got the worst bed again." Tess continued, sinking her weight on it. "Anybody got snuff?"

Nobody had, and Maria said rather testily: "Do you think you could get yourself to bed, so that we could go back to sleep soon?"

"Wha' a welcome," was the reply, before the candle was put out and she stretched on the bed fully dressed and fell asleep.

The following morning Penny very carefully ironed her dress. It was the only fine thing, or indeed the only garment, she owned. She'd have to take the seams out again soon, and she smiled at her own canniness in having had Madame de Chantal use more material than necessary.

Frederick had said the lilac suited her colouring. He'd congratulated her on her good taste.

'I'm not going to think about him,' she thought, as usual feeling a fire of fury in her heart whenever he surfaced. She brought the dress upstairs and placed it underneath her mattress carefully folded. Here, it would be out of sight until she got a chance to adjust it.

Later that day, Tess was missing.

"She's stolen something, and made off with it afore anybody notices," said Maria.

Some women patted lockets around their necks, reassuring themselves they were still there. Penny was wearing her only bracelet, a gold one given her by Martin Eglinton.

It was later that night, before she went to bed, that she peeped under her mattress to make sure her dress had not crumpled. But her dress was gone.

"That varmint!" she said aloud, indignant. "She went off with my gown!"

"Oh and that was a nice one," said Julia with sympathy. "You shoulda put it on you immediately, you know? She had the cleanin' of the room this morning, so she upended the mattresses."

"It was the only one I had," Penny was very angry. "I have a good mind to go to the police!"

But the others laughed. "You won't get any satisfaction from the police," said one. "Was it really yours anyway?" Maria teased. They knew she'd had a fancy-man.

Penny, however, would not be appeased. She was furious. She now owned nothing, not even the clothes on her back. Only her bracelet.

CHAPTER FIFTY-FOUR

Penny was thinking, more and more that she would return to Manchester as Bernice had suggested. Surely the Eglintons would not turn away an innocent child! Perhaps she would approach Matilda Valley.

She had to find money to return to Manchester, but how to do that? Perhaps she should write first. Oh dear, she hadn't written to Mamma in an age! She resolved to do that before she approached the Eglintons. Perhaps her mother might send her money, for the fare North, if she had any.

Mornings in the Shelter were spent working, and it was hard work to keep the house clean as a pin. The rooms were small, and had to be turned out daily. The hall and parlours were cleaned and polished. Ironing was done daily, there was a great deal of mending, and the large upstairs cupboards always had folded sheets and pillow-cases ready to be put on beds.

Women came and went. Occasionally a man came to the door, sober and contrite, and would be admitted to the parlour for a lecture by Bernice, who was a great scolder when the occasion demanded. Only then was the contrite husband allowed to see his wife, and she often left with him, but sometimes refused. Sometimes Mick O'Hara had to be called upon to remove a reluctant husband. There was no provision for children at the Shelter so most of the women were either unwed, newly married, or their children had grown up and gone away. Some, like Penny, had been abandoned by a lover, and there were a few women with child as she was.

In the late afternoon, after the work was finished, the women were free to do as they pleased before it was time to cook and wash dishes afterward and lay the tables for breakfast. Many chose to sit and sew for expected babies, their own or others. Penny liked to go out and walk around the streets. She had no love for the crowded, smelly places but was hungry for something, some idea, or an inspiration that waited for her somewhere outside the Shelter. Thoughts and ideas were free, and she had plenty of them. But to have no money! It was intolerable. She'd have to find permanent work, as a companion again perhaps, and of course, she would have to pass herself off as a widow the next time. But who would welcome a woman with a baby?

One day, she passed an old second-hand bookshop. How she loved, and missed books! She had no money, but browsing was free. She moved about, picking up a book here and there, looking at it, before replacing it on the shelf.

"See anything you like, Miss?" asked the bookseller.

"I see plenty of what I like, but I have no money to spare on books just now," she said.

"Feel free to browse then. I don't mind. You're not from around 'ere, are you?" he asked.

"No, from Manchester."

"Manchester! Now that's an interesting thing. There's news from Manchester today. In the paper. Do you happen to know Clifton?"

"I do – what of it?"

"A house burned down to the ground in Clifton a few days ago."

"Where in Clifton? Does it say? Do you have the newspaper?"

He handed her his copy, opening the page and pointing out the article.

She read:

Fire engulfed a house last night in the Clifton Walk area of Manchester. All were saved, except a crippled member of the family, name of Eglinton, who was rescued but who died two days later from his burns. The cause of the fire is unknown.

A deep despair and sorrow overwhelmed her. The bookseller saw her distress and hurriedly brought a chair.

"Sit down, Miss. You knew them, did you? Knew them well? I am sorry for your loss. Were they kin? Shall I get you a glass of water?" He hurried off to the room at the back.

Penny's head swam. *Martin was dead.* She could not believe it, could not grasp it, could not comprehend that her darling Martin was no longer on this earth. She would never see him again; her child would never know his father!

The world had suddenly become a different place.

The water was put to her lips by the shopkeeper's wife. She drank without even knowing.

"What was 'e to you, dearie?" she asked gently.

"He was my husband," she said. "Yes, he was. My husband."

She burst into great sobs.

CHAPTER FIFTY-FIVE

Mr. Wells was a man of principle. Where had Miss Fowler, or Mrs.Eglinton, gone? She had no family in London.

Sometimes, it was necessary to ask the servants, who always seemed to know more than their employers. He asked everyone who worked in the house, ending with the footmen and the coachman.

The coachman, Noone, had some very pertinent information. A gentleman had come about the Chiswick taverns some time ago, and asked questions about Miss Fowler. He'd been directed to him.

"What did you say?"

"I said she was taken on in Manchester as companion to Mrs. Wells, and that after a short time, she 'ad been dismissed because she was in a pregnant condition."

"How did you know that she was in a - delicate - condition?" asked Mr. Wells.

The coachman gave him a withering look. "I don't rightly know, sir, but everybody knew that's why she got dismissed. Rightly so, too, sir."

"Who was this gentleman?"

"He was a Mr. Butler, and 'is coachman says he come from Park Street."

"Thank you, Noone, and it would behove you and the other servants not to gossip so much." said Mr. Wells with severity.

"Yes, sir," said Noone, thinking that it was rather pathetic of the Master to come to him for information and then scold him for having it.

"Now if you would put the horses to, I will proceed to Park Street, and you shall find out the house."

"Yes, sir."

A short time later he was being shown into Mr. Butler's fine drawing room.

"I have no idea where she went, Mr. Wells. She was here to help the housekeeper with some extra sewing or mending or something. According to Mrs. Perkins, she disappeared. I heard things of her subsequently that were not too flattering." Mr. Butler was annoyed. When a girl was out of his life, he never wanted to hear of her again. "You might try Spitalfields."

But Mr. Wells decided that it was not feasible to go searching in London's vice-filled quarters.

"I would be obliged to you to pass on the word to your housekeeper, that if any of your household has any contact with her, she should come and see me. I am always home in the evenings. I wish to tell her of the sad death of her mother. I also wish – but as to that, never mind." Mr. Wells wanted to give her some money, to make up for her sad treatment at the hands of his mother, enough to get her back home.

Mr. Butler made his promises, and Harkness saw him out.

He could not get Penelope from his head for the rest of the day. Her mother was dead. He'd never thought of her having a mother, or a father, or anybody. He had never asked her about them and if she began to talk of any family member, or anything about Manchester, he'd shut her up in that way he had, of looking around with impatience and tapping his fingers against each other. To him, Penelope – or any of the women with whom he was involved - was not really a human being. He was angry that she had surfaced as one.

CHAPTER FIFTY-SIX

As Mr. Butler sat in his smoking jacket that evening, enjoying a port, the doorbell rang. He was surprised to see a policeman shown in. His visitor had a very odd story, and as he listened, his heart seethed in annoyance.

It seemed that the night before, a young woman had been drinking in The Ten Bells in Spitalfields, and had left the tavern in an inebriated condition. A coach and four was turning the corner, and the woman, crossing the street, had been thrown under the horses' hooves. She had not had anything upon her to identify her, except the signature of a noted couturier sewn into the bodice of her gown –CdeC.

They had visited Madame de Chantal. She had come to the morgue with great reluctance, and had been unable to identify the body of the young woman, but knew that she had made the lilac dress with the three puce stripes down the front for a Miss Fowler of Park Street, and Mr. F. Butler was to receive the bill. She had broken down in tears and said that yes, it was Miss Fowler – and then – no, it was not Miss

Fowler. She did not know, she could not say, not for sure – but maybe yes, oh her face, her poor face!

The police requested Mr. Butler to come and identify the body.

Butler tried to beg off. It would be a task he utterly detested, but the policeman was firm, so he had to go to the Morgue. He entered, hating the smell of decaying corpses and heavy antiseptic, trying not to see the forms under the sheets. He was taken to one. The sheet was lifted, he turned and almost became sick. The woman's face had been trampled upon and was unrecognisable. Fair hair, like Penny's, tumbled about her shoulders.

"I don't know," he said, in great irritation.

The policeman whipped the sheet off completely, and he too recognised the dress. Why had Madame woman hesitated? Hysterical woman, if she'd had her head about her, she could have said *yes* and be done with it.

"It is Miss Fowler," he snarled. "Now may I go?"

He felt ill as he walked out the door and into the fresh air. Had she committed suicide? She should have gone to work for Mrs. Dooley, stupid woman! He did everything to fend off the guilt he felt welling up in him.

The newest mistress was waiting for him when he returned, but he curtly told her to leave. He gave her money. He wished to be alone. Miss Fowler had ruined everything for him. He'd go to Switzerland alone.

He would tell nobody, not Perkins, nor any of the servants, that Miss Fowler had met her end. He felt that they would blame him, unfairly. They need not know. He hoped her name would not appear in the papers. He would contact his lawyer immediately to put a stop to that, in case his name should appear.

CHAPTER FIFTY-SEVEN

Mr. Wells postponed the sad duty of writing back to the Reverend to tell him that he had not found Miss Fowler, or Mrs. Eglinton, as he preferred to think of her now. Her sad situation, and the cruel treatment she had received from his mother, was preying on his mind.

He had never married. An intensely shy man, not handsome, and very bookish, he had never wooed a girl, except from afar. He'd written poems to a Miss Havers, a Miss Plunkett and a Miss Sharpe, and though he had received scrawled notes of *thank yous for the pretty verses,* they were always about to go abroad, or visit an aunt in Scotland, or had a severe cold if he asked to call upon them.

Alas! Miss Fowler – or Mrs. Eglinton? Which? It mattered not. He was determined to assist her. He fancied himself gallant, and there was a lady in deep distress. He therefore returned to his favourite source for news – the servants. He bid his coachman, Noone, to go back to Park Street and ask pertinent questions of the staff at Mr. Butler's.

"You know I shall 'ave to gossip," said Noone with sarcasm.

"It is in a good cause," said Mr. Wells, giving him ten shillings to buy drinks in a tavern for whoever was willing to talk. He sighed. Why was most of London's business done in taverns?

Noone had news for him the following day. It had been an easy matter to find out that Mr. Butler's coachman had driven Miss Fowler to Dicey Dooley's at Spitalfields. Noone had taken it upon himself to visit Dicey Dooley's establishment. A dreadful place. Raucous, immoral, vice-ridden! And they had never heard of her, but a woman named Julia had said Miss Fowler was at the Distressed Woman's Shelter in Devon Street.

"And that's where she is." said Noone with satisfaction.

"Well done, Noone!"

Mr. Wells made his way to Spitalfields the very next day, and found the Women's Shelter.

CHAPTER FIFTY-EIGHT

"What do you want?" snapped Mrs. O'Hara, surveying the man in front of her. Whose husband was this middle-aged well-got up gent, she wondered? Not Maria. Nor Thelma, who was only seventeen. What about the new one from last night, the Russian named Olga?

"I was hoping to see Miss Fowler," he said with some timidity.

"Oh, do come in," she said graciously, but rather disappointed she had nobody to scold. This was not the fancy-man that threw his discarded women to Dicey Dooley.

"Mr. Wells!" said Penny in surprise when she entered.

"Miss Fowler – or is it Mrs. Eglinton?" he said.

Penny motioned to him to sit down.

"How do you know I am – or was – Mrs. Eglinton?"

"Your grandmother is looking for you. She asked her clergyman to write. She wished to impart the very sad news to you – of your mother's untimely death of pneumonia. I am sorry, Mrs. Eglinton. Deeply sorry." He said, leaning forward, as Penny buried her head in her hands in grief.

"Mrs. Eglinton – "

"Why do you keep calling me Mrs. Eglinton?" she asked him. "The marriage was annulled, and in any case – " she burst into fresh tears.

He drew out the letter from his inside pocket and she read it. But instead of hope in her eyes, fresh tears came.

"He is dead since this letter was written – dead in a fire, Mr. Wells."

"Oh my poor dear Mrs. Eglinton!" cried the gentleman with feeling. "This is truly dreadful, for I fear that you loved him."

"I did!" she said with heartbreak. "I should never have left Manchester."

"Upon that subject, Mrs, Eglinton, I am deeply sorry that it is upon our account that you have come to this place. First, you take shelter with the Mr. Butler's household, sewing, I understand, and you suddenly vanished from there, you fled perhaps? The treatment you received in my mother's house (for it is hers, not mine) was abhorrent. I wish to make it up to you. If you will, I wish to grant you some recompense for what was done, by giving you a sum of money, enough to take you back to Manchester, if that is what you wish to do, and I think you should, for even though Mr. Eglinton is dead, and your mother also - your grandmother may have need of you, and no doubt the Eglinton family would like to take you into their care, considering - ." He took an envelope from his pocket. "Here is fifty pounds."

"You are kind, Mr. Wells!" she said, taking it gladly. "I will go back to Manchester!"

"Is there anything else I can do for you, Mrs. Eglinton?"

She hesitated.

"You were correct when I said I had to flee Park Street. I had no opportunity to recover my clothes and other possessions. I would be very grateful if you could try to get them for me."

"It is as good as done, Mrs. Eglinton." said the gentleman.

Penny spent the next days in grief. She remembered how good her mother was, how she was never afraid of plain speaking, and she remembered especially her charitable heart. As long as she lived, she'd never be as good as Mamma. Worst of all, she'd never see her again!

CHAPTER FIFTY-NINE

Mr. Butler had no peace, none. He felt ill. He refused food. He was sick in his stomach, in his head, everywhere. He went to bed, he could not sleep; he got up and felt exhausted. He was liverish, feverish, snappish. He walked about the house, pacing his own rooms, and avoiding the French bedchamber. He could not even look in the direction of the door. He refused invitations, turned away his barber and his tailor when they called; he drank. He muttered to himself. The servants were worried.

Finally he wrote a letter to the Eglinton family and sealed it. He gave it to his footman to post. Then he locked his bedroom door and said he was not to be disturbed. He stayed there for two days.

But on the evening of the second day the doorbell echoed through the house, and the butler said that Mr. Wells was downstairs and insisted upon seeing him. He refused.

Then he heard Mr. Wells voice outside his own chamber, and the knocking began, upon his own door!

"If you will not see me, then please give an order for Mrs. Perkins to pack Mrs. Eglinton's clothes! Surely it cannot be that difficult! Are you unwell, man? This is ridiculous. What's the matter with you?"

"Who wants her clothes?" retorted Butler.

"Why, she does, of course! She as much as told me that she hasn't a stitch to wear but what's on her back!"

"What? She'd dead, you fool!"

"She's not dead, and you're the fool!"

Mr. Wells was quite enjoying himself. Nothing this dramatic had ever happened him before.

The door opened suddenly.

"She's – she's not dead?" Butler's voice was a squeak.

"Goodness, man! What is wrong with you? You look as if you haven't slept for weeks, and you're unwashed, and your shirt is hanging out. Do you need a doctor?"

"She's not dead?"

"She is not dead and she wants her clothes and all her belongings! She said she would like to send the dress back, one that was belonging to somebody in this house - another servant perhaps - I am sure your housekeeper will know more than you about that - but it was stolen by a woman who took shelter in the same house as she. Pray inform the housekeeper!"

"Mrs. Perkins! Mrs. Perkins!" shouted the unkempt man, staggering out onto the landing.

CHAPTER SIXTY

Mr. Eglinton was buried and the sad troupe returned to the Valley house. They all had their memories; even Mrs. Eglinton remembered something good about her husband, before he had become avaricious, he had had a pleasant enough way about him.

His lawyer, Mr. Creighton, produced the will. His affairs were in some disorder, and it would take some time to untangle them. His study in Eglinton House was in ashes, every paper and receipt gone. At least the house was insured, but the Eglinton family would have to live very modestly from now on. Martin had inherited shares in his father's companies, a rather odd bequest considering he was supposed to be out of his mind. The factories and the shipping line was going through a difficult time.

Martin was recovering in his sister's house. His face was burned on the left side, and his left hand was still swathed in bandages. Dressing changes were very painful, and healing would be slow. It seemed to Martin that he had exchanged one handicap only to be supplied with another, for he did not know if he would regain the use of his left hand again. As for his face, there would be scarring, but he was not very vain, and a clever arrangement of his hair might cover most of it. It was fortunately fashionable for a man to sport sideburns. Martin was used to misfortune, and he was glad to be alive, and to have walked to the extent of being able to rescue his father was a triumph for him.

Miss Kent visited from her home in Bolton, but was seen less often as Martin's financial prospects became less certain.

"I thought she liked you," Mrs. Eglinton said, rather annoyed. She wanted Martin to be happy with a woman who loved him dearly, would be devoted to him, and not mind his poverty, if it came to that. She had hardly dared to think of her own future – it was too soon – she was in mourning clothes. Dr. Aldridge – Michael – had been her friend for many years.

"Mother, we have to engage some doctors to declare me fit and sane," Martin reminded her. "There is no future for me, if this stands, in a professional or a personal life."

"Without delay," she promised. "What is it, Joan?" The maid had brought in a letter addressed to Mr. Eglinton.

"That is I, now," said Martin, taking it. "From London! Could it be Penny? Not her hand, it is a man's hand." He frowned.

"Her employer, perhaps." Said his mother, looking over his shoulder.

Martin opened the envelope and took out the sheet of fine notepaper. He became pale as he read it.

"What is it, Martin?"

"Read it, it was meant for you and Papa." His face was almost as white as his bandages, his eyes staring.

Dear Mr. & Mrs. Eglinton,

I have unfortunate news with which you should be acquainted. Your former daughter-in-law, Mrs. Martin Eglinton, has had a fatal accident, involving a coach and four, on May 1st last. She was attempting to cross the street and it came around a corner at such a pace, that the accident was unavoidable. She was killed instantly and I am assured by the police that she did not suffer.

Mrs. Martin Eglinton was a member of my household for a time before this, under the guidance of my housekeeper, gaining skills as a seamstress, which is why I was appraised of the sad facts after it happened. Another fact of which you ought to be aware is that, and this is particularly painful to relate – she was to have a child.

It gives me great heartache to relate this news. I myself was called upon by the police to identify her. She is buried in Claxtonbury cemetery.

Yours, etc,

Frederick Butler.

CHAPTER SIXTY-ONE

Penny believed that Martin died in the fire at Eglinton House; and the identification of Miss Tess Barton's body as that of Penelope's by Mr. Butler had made its way to Martin. It all might have been resolved very speedily, in Penny's return to Manchester as she planned, but for a circumstance that occurred in Crumpsall Workhouse. The Reverend Parry informed the ailing Mrs. Pyke that her granddaughter was found, and that she was well. Mrs. Pyke was very happy to hear it, a great peace came over her, and she passed away in her sleep. After the Reverend had done his duty in yet another sad letter to London, he put the matter out of his mind, as he had the Bishop coming and was behindhand with the preparations.

When Penny received this news some days later, conveyed by Mr. Wells by the second letter from Reverend Parry, she could hardly bear it. Still housed at the shelter, she had Mrs. O'Hara and the other women to comfort her.

There was no reason for her now to return to Manchester ever again. The only family member she had in the world was her unborn baby, and she would never part from this child, no matter what happened. The baby was a part of Martin, and she lavished love upon this little one whose little kicks reminded her of his coming. The other women were good company and great counsel. Many were very poor and illiterate, she was teaching them how to read and write. They helped and supported each other and she was content to stay there until it was time for her to go to the Charitable Infirmary run by the Society for Distressed Women. What a great thing it was that people with means were able to give to those without.

Penny told nobody about the money she had been given, and hid it carefully upon her person. She kept change in her outside pocket to give to the many emaciated children she met on her daily walk, or to careworn, hollowed-eyed mothers. She walked humbly along, remembering her resolution, grateful for what she had and trying not to fear the future.

CHAPTER SIXTY-TWO

Mr. Wells had polished his little speech. It was not the speech he intended to make to Penelope for her hand. It was a speech to another. There was a formidable obstacle in his path; not that of her carrying another man's child; nor her poverty; nor the difference in their ages (he was forty-eight); but his mother. Although she accepted now that Penny had not been in disgrace, and was sorry for it, and had even sent her a letter of apology and some money, she had formed the idea that Percy would never marry, and was quite cheered by the thought that no other woman would replace her. Her failing sight also meant that he would be devoted to her all her life.

Mr. Wells paced up and down the drawing room before dinner. His mother was expected down any time and he had decided that he was going to speak tonight.

She came in, her step slow and careful, and found her way to her own chair, the winged tapestried Queen Anne by the mantelpiece.

He cleared his throat and sat on his chair opposite, which matched hers. It had been his father's chair long ago.

"Mother," he began. "I have something I wish to tell you."

"You're getting married, aren't you?"

He was taken aback.

"How do you know?"

"I might be going blind, but I know when your attention is elsewhere. You're taken up with this unfortunate woman in every conversation we have. I do not have any objection. You love her, and I'm not quite as selfish as you think."

"Mother! How generous of you!" he sprang from his chair and embraced her.

"But I do want you to think of a rather serious aspect of the entire affair."

"What is that, Mother?!"

"The marriage must not take place until after the child is born."

"What? Mother! I mean to save her from her disgrace, of the perception of it, for most people think she is unmarried!"

"Percy, I beg you to listen to me. If you marry her before she has the child, your name will be on the birth certificate as the father. If it is a boy, and then you have a boy of your own, what a mess it would be! For her boy, who has no connection with our family, would be legally your heir. Have you thought of it?"

"I have not, Mother. I am glad you mention it. It is a grave consideration. If only we could know if it were a boy or a girl!"

"That's impossible. There are all sorts of old wives tales, a great deal of heartburn predicts a girl, and carrying the child low predicts a boy. None of it is true. And Percy – there's another aspect of this I am sure you've never considered."

Percy looked at her dumbly, his elation draining by the minute.

"When you marry, it would be very unwise to take the child in, even if your name is not on the birth certificate."

"Whyever not, Mother? May I not even raise the fatherless child as my son?"

"Certainly not. There will be expectations on his part. He will feel he is heir to this house and to our estate in Yorkshire. There will be trouble between him and his step-brother. He must be sent back to the Eglintons."

Percy resumed his pacing.

"So I should not marry until after the baby is born, and if it's a boy, he will not come here. If it's a girl?"

"In principle, she has no claim on us either, for her maintenance and education, but if her mother makes a horrid fuss, she may come here, I suppose. But, her mother will insist upon her being known as Miss Wells, not Miss Eglinton, for that would be a complicated thing to have to explain to everybody. And as Miss Wells, she will take precedence over your own daughters wherever they go."

Percy sat heavily on his chair again.

"It all seems very complicated," he said.

"It is complicated indeed!" said his mother, trying to watch his expression. His head, hung low, gave her hope. She did not want him to marry. She was old and did not want a young woman and a young family in the house. If he did marry, she would move to a smaller house, with her own staff, but she did not wish to do that. Her own convenience was more important to her than her son's chance of happiness, and then his renewed hopes of having a family to be his joy in his old age.

"It might be better not to marry her at all." he said flatly.

The door opened and the footman announced dinner. Percy helped his mother up from the chair and took her into the dining-room. He did not say a word throughout dinner and his disappointment was evident to her. She felt pangs of guilt, but what she had done was for the best. She was sure it would have been a very unhappy union in any case, as the woman was so below her son in every way.

CHAPTER SIXTY-THREE

Mrs. Eglinton and Martin removed to a house some miles from Clifton Walk on Newcastle Road, which they had to rent until the insurance claim was settled. It was a modest two-storey set in a small park, in an area where doctors and lawyers and business people were building at a fast rate. Martin was muddling through his late father's businesses, there had been small improvements of late, and he had some hope of financial solvency.

"I wonder how are things at Regents Court?" mused Martin one day as he and his mother ate dinner. "Penny's mother and grandmother must be devastated as we are, by her loss."

"When we were at Clifton Walk, Betty used to bring us news. Now we have no connection there at all." said his mother. She privately thought that Penny never paid her family enough attention as she had come up in the world. It did not say much for her character. She'd been so ready to believe Penny was perfect, for she had been so grateful that she'd married Martin! But then her improved circumstances had gone completely to her head. And not for a moment did Mrs. Eglinton believe that she had been a *seamstress* in Mr. Butler's household! Not after the rumours which had circulated about them in Manchester! Indeed! But Martin had loved her deeply and mourned her, and the child that they were going to have. Mrs. Eglinton did not doubt it was an Eglinton child; she did not believe that Penny had done anything more than taken a few walks with Butler.

She rightly supposed that after she went to London and found she was with child, she had run to Butler hoping his attentions had meant he was in love with her.

Even Martin had admitted to her that he doubted the seamstress story, and thought that Penny may have been desperate enough to give herself to Mr. Butler, who everybody knew was a rake.

Privately, Mrs. Eglinton wondered about the carriage accident. Had Penny taken her own life after revealing her condition? Butler would not have taken the news of her expected child well. Poor Penny! She hoped she had not done that. Where there was life, there was always hope. She would cease these morbid thoughts, and look to the future.

"Dr. Aldridge has arranged to have you visited by a Drs. Farquhar and Lowell, both mental specialists." She said, then. "It's dreadful you have to go through this again."

"Mother, you can call Dr. Aldridge *Michael*, to me. I know how it is between you," Martin smiled, a rare occurrence since the devastating letter from Frederick Butler.

His mother blushed and looked at her plate.

"I told him it was hopeless, you know. That he should go away and meet other people, other women, find himself a nice wife and have a family. He came close to it once or twice, even became engaged, but ended it. I was disappointed for him. Oh, Martin – let me cut that for you - "

"No, Mother," he said with firmness. "I have to learn to do things with one hand, and the other helping as best it can. I have hopes that it will come around."

After a moment, he said:

"Now you are free, Mother, to seek your own happiness."

"Oh, son, you would not disapprove? There is a period of mourning of course, but after that... I shall be Mrs. Aldridge then. You would not mind?"

"Mother! Of course I would not mind! Nor would Matilda."

"You and Matilda do not think it an insult to your late father that I should be so disposed?"

"No, Mamma." Martin wondered if it was time to tell his mother about Peru. He related it in full. His mother listened, distressed. How had Martin kept this from her, for so long? His own father the cause of his illness! And the slave trade that hardly anybody in England knew about, or there would have been public outrage! How cruel!

Silence fell as they sat in the drawing room. The dusk was coming earlier and outside their window, leaves whirled about. They did not talk. It was usually like this. Martin was lost in his own thoughts. His mother wondered how it would be, when she became Mrs. Aldridge. Martin would be alone. Would he ever marry again? She mentioned it, delicately.

"I always had hope that Penny and I would be remarried," he said quietly. "But she is gone forever, and so is my joy in life."

"Time will heal." his mother said quietly. "In another few years, you may find yourself able to begin again."

"I have had plenty of practise in new beginnings," he said. "I have learned not to fear them."

CHAPTER SIXTY-FOUR

"**H**e was sweet on you, that little guvnor," said Pauline, glibly, as she and Penny sewed together one day. "We all thought 'e was going to propose marriage to you! Did 'e not?"

"No, and it was just as well, for I would have refused."

"What! Refused a good home for you and your child! All the fancy things you'd 'ave 'ad, I woulda said Yes, I would, if he 'ad asked me!"

"I married once for security and wealth, and look where it got me." said Penny.

"You said you fell in love with Mr. Eglinton in the end." Pauline pointed out.

"Yes, but his family didn't like me. His father contrived me to go." Penny wasn't sure she was using the word 'contrive' the correct way. But what did it matter?

"There's only the old woman you'd 'ave 'ad to deal wiv," said Pauline, holding up a piece of linen and frowning at it, squinting. "How does a pillowcase get rents in it? What sharp pieces are there in somebody's ears? Bella Atkins went to bed with 'er hairpins, that's it, an' they poked thru' 'er nightcap. That's who should have the mending of this."

"I won't live in a house with that harridan Mrs. Wells." Penny continued. "She rules her son. Oh she wrote me a very pretty letter an' all, apologising, but I'm never going back there, ever. She made me feel like a piece of dirt, and that doctor she got to examine me, I was never so humiliated in my life. She knew what was up with me afore she got the doctor, I'm sure of it!"

But Pauline was not listening. "Bella!" she cried, as she saw the girl pass the door. A quarrel ensued as Bella said that Pauline was raving. Mick O'Hara's dog had pulled it from the clothesline. Hairpins indeed! Now would Pauline like to say she was sorry?

Penny would have enjoyed the quarrel, but she felt a sudden pain in her lower stomach. She put down her sewing.

The girls continued their quarrel until they heard Penny cry out suddenly. The quarrel was forgotten; they were at her side in an instant.

CHAPTER SIXTY-FIVE

Penny's baby son was born early the following morning in the Charitable Infirmary. As she had dropped her maiden name in full, she named him Martin Harold Eglinton. She herself would be known to anybody she introduced herself to as Mrs. Eglinton, a widow, whose child was born *posthumously*. The doctor had given her the word posthumous. It was a fine big word and she intended to use it. He said she'd done very well, and only looked in on her after it was all over.

"I thought I was going to die," she remarked to the midwife as she took her child in her arms. She'd certainly never worked so hard in her life before, but upon looking at the sweet baby face, and the tiny fist curled around her finger, she reckoned he was worth it.

He was a handsome child, with a head of dark hair, his father's high forehead and his look about his mouth and chin. Penny could not take her eyes off her beautiful son.

Someday, she'd take him back to Manchester to show Martin's family. But she was still terribly afraid of the power that the old man had over the Eglintons. He could not harm Martin now, he was at rest, but he could harm her. He could take the child away from her; people with money, power and connections could do as much evil as they liked, it seemed, while people like her, poor and without patronage, were helpless.

For now, it was better they did not know of little Marty.

She had to find a way to provide for him, though. She prayed about it, and over the next few days asked everybody on the staff in the Hospital if anybody needed a seamstress to live-in. The doctor promised he's ask his wife to ask her friends, but nothing was coming of that.

The baby cried, and she put him to nurse.

"Lord, thank You for the gift of little Martin. Our circumstances are bad, but You will help us, and I will work hard. Wealth and fine clothes don't mean anything to me now. I've learned that. Please put some work my way."

Many women like her went to the Workhouse. She was not going to do that.

Some days after her child was born, she had an unexpected, if rather unwelcome, visitor. Mr. Wells brought his mother to see her.

She peered into the cradle and admired the fine head of hair, and asked Penny how she was going to provide for him?

"I don't know," she admitted. She half-feared that Mr. Wells would propose to her there in the Ward, he was looking at her with a sort of grave tenderness, as if she was his responsibility.

"I have been making particular enquiries upon your behalf, Mrs. Eglinton. There is a Mrs. Galsworthy with whom I am acquainted whose daughter, Mrs. Gordon, is in need of a housekeeper. We have told her of your misfortune, of losing your husband and having a child to care for. She is fond of children and does not object to an infant in arms. She lives in Brighton. A very pretty place, you know, with healthy air for the child. She will pay you ten pounds a year, all found. What do you say?"

Brighton! A place by the sea! All found! No objection to a child! But this from Mrs. Wells, from whom she did not want any favours, Mrs. Wells, whose barbs she had not forgotten, and certainly not forgiven!

"Mother has gone to great trouble to find you a place," Mr. Wells said with eagerness.

She swallowed.

"What do you say, Mrs. Eglinton?" rapped Mrs. Wells. She looked rather offended already, awaiting her answer. How Penny would love to say no, and offend her even more!

Lord, help me, she said a silent prayer.

It came upon her with swiftness that this was the answer to her prayer! God has sent her arch-enemy with the solution to her pressing circumstances. It would have to be 'Yes.' Even though she disliked this woman, she now had her baby to think of, and this situation seemed like a God sent one.

"I am delighted to accept," she said. "Forgive me, I was dumfounded! I prayed for a suitable situation!"

She saw Mrs. Wells' face soften.

"I don't believe in prayers and suchlike," she said briskly. "But I think that you could not do better than this. Poor Mrs. Gordon cannot have any children, and your child will gladden her heart. Shall I tell her, then, that it will be a settled thing?"

"Please do!"

"You will not be expected to take up your duties for six weeks at least, so I suggest you come to us in the meantime." Said Mrs. Wells. "I shall set you some light work, and you shall have time with your child, as he needs it. There is an old nursery room, you may have that, and sit there with him. You can be sure of a fire every day. You will take your meals in the servant's hall."

All the time she spoke, her son nodded his agreement.

Penny could hardly believe her ears at the kind offer. When they left, she lay back on the pillow and stared at the ceiling for a long time, thinking about how God surprises people, and how He uses even people that one dislikes to bring answers!

CHAPTER SIXTY-SIX

Martin walked with Miss Kent up the driveway of the house he was thinking of purchasing just outside Manchester. They had alighted the carriage outside the gate, the better to examine the approach to the front door. He walked very well now, with a cane, and could manage a mile without tiring. His mother had remarried over a year ago as soon as her period of mourning was over, and moved into the Doctor's house.

The front garden was neat, and spring blossoms peeked from the hedges on this April day.

"Do you like it?" he asked, somewhat shyly. "It's a bit old-fashioned perhaps."

"It is smaller than I imagined," she replied in a disappointed voice. "Is this to be our permanent residence?"

"I think of it as such," he said.

"It puts me in mind of one of those roomy picturesque cottages the Regency peers were very fond of." Miss Kent went on. "But none ever lived in them; they went there to play at being cottagers, and would invite an intimate circle of friends for an informal dinner party with dancing for six or seven couples, at the most."

"With seven bedrooms, this house is surely larger than a cottage," Martin said. "The agent did not describe it as such, indeed. Well, shall we see inside?" He took out the front door key.

The interior did not put Miss Kent into better humour.

"The hallway is poky, and I dislike the flooring."

She swept into the drawing room.

"It is not spacious enough, it has a closed feel. The light is poor. And I so dislike a blue marble fireplace; it would have to be taken out and another put in, at enormous expense."

Every room had a major fault, and it was evident that the future Mrs. Eglinton would be dreadfully unhappy living in this particular house. They went out the kitchen door.

"Such a scrawny walled garden! Overall, the park this house sits in is very small. There's no pond."

"Small! It is larger than that of Eglinton House!"

"But you have to consider what I am used to, Martin."

Martin walked back out with her, silent. Miss Kent's airs got on his nerves. Because her father had a knighthood, she felt that she was continually being observed and judged by everybody. His own mother and sister had reversed their good opinion of her. Unfortunately, their names were now firmly linked and he would be seen as a cad if he broke off their engagement.

"You're not speaking to me, Martin," she said, tucking her arm in his. "Are you sulking?"

"No, not sulking, just thinking."

"I hate it when you think. Why can you not talk to me? When you are quiet, I always wonder if I have said something wrong."

"I'm not a prate, Alice. You have to get used to my thinking, my silences."

Martin sunk even more into silence. His thoughts turned again to Penny, his dear wife, now dead. She was chatty, but did not mind when he was not, and never fretted that she was to blame if he was in a quiet mood. Penny, for all her faults – and he could see them in hindsight – avarice, for one – did not fretfully demand attention as Miss Kent.

"You're thinking of her, aren't you? The laundry woman."

"That woman was my wife." said Martin.

"No. She was not, really not your wife. But she will always be between us, will she not? You have to make up your mind, Martin. You have had a diagnosis of insanity – now lifted, I know, but it will not be forgotten by everybody, and will be whispered of for years to come. This I am willing to put up with, the whispers and innuendo, and everybody watching us."

"Put up with!" Martin felt angry.

"I did not mean it the way it sounded," Miss Kent said. "But Penny is dead, and you have to put her out of your mind, if you want a life with me. I want you to forget her, for she was, you must admit, a dreadful mistake. Your mother has admitted her regret about the affair. Cut that part of your life away."

"Penny was the reason I dragged myself out of bed and onto my feet."

"She has fulfilled her function then. Now she's dead. Forget her, will you? Do you not love me, Martin?" she added in a fretful voice.

"Yes, I do, Alice." But Martin wondered again what it was about Alice he loved. Her appearance was excellent, her need of him flattering, but her manner and personality very grating sometimes, and he seemed to so easily offend her that he was not at all sure they would be happy.

"And you will tell the agent to find us a bigger, more stately house? Come, Martin, you must look at properties that are more fitting for your position in life. Your position as head of Eglinton Imports demands it. Let us not quarrel. In twelve weeks, we'll be husband and wife!"

She tucked her head against his shoulder and he patted her hand.

"Next Tuesday, I leave for London," she said gaily then. "My mother and I are to shop, and we have engaged to have my new gowns made by *Maison de Chantal*. It is said to be the very best! Say you will join us there, Martin! We will stay at Claridges.

CHAPTER SIXTY-SEVEN

"**M**arty! Marty!" The little boy turned at the sound of his name, and upon feet that were growing more steady by the day, ran to his mother who was at the back door. She swept him up in her arms and he laughed.

"What have you been doing down in the mud? What a dirty face!" she said, swinging him about as he chortled. "And what have you got in your hand?"

"Present for Mamma!" he said, glowing, opening his hand to reveal a rather dazed worm.

"Ooh that's very kind of you, Marty, but we 'ave to put 'im back, because worms like to be in the garden!"

"Worms nice!"

"Oh, very nice! But it's time for your milk." Penny shook the worm from his little hand and carried him into the kitchen and taking a rag, dipped it in soapy water and wiped his face and hands.

"I declare I don't know you," she said with great fondness. "What's yer name? Tell me."

"Marty Add Egton." He said with pride.

"Martin Harold Eglinton." She touched the tip of his nose.

"And where does Mamma come from?"

"Manchy."

"Manchester, Mamma comes from Manchester!"

"Manchy!"

"And where is your Papa?"

"Papa 'Eaven," he said, with solemnity, joining his hands as if in prayer.

"Yes, Papa's in Heaven."

"Manchy 'Eaven," he said then.

"What a funny thing to say, love!" Penny kissed the top of his head and gave him a cup of milk.

She put him to bed some time later, and in the candlelight, after kissing him goodnight, watched his chubby angelic cheeks, and his dark curl over his forehead, and his fist curled under his chin. She went back down to the kitchen, there to finish up some work and then she would read for a while before going up to bed, in the bed beside her baby's cot. He would sleep all night, and be awake before her in the morning, all chirpy and smiling at her.

The parlour maid came to the kitchen and told her she was wanted upstairs. This was unusual, and she became a little concerned as to her situation. She was confident of doing a very good job, and her child did not get in the way of her duties, for the couple seemed to like him very much, and were very understanding if he was ill and she needed to be with him. Mrs. Gordon herself sometimes took him for walks around the garden and amused him. What a dreadful pity they did not have any children themselves! Her mistress loved children.

Mr. and Mrs. Gordon were in the drawing room. She thought that Mrs. Gordon looked nervous. She was bidden to be seated.

"This is a little awkward, Mrs. Eglinton. And I do not quite know how to broach it." Began Mr. Gordon, who was obviously going to be the spokesman. Penny felt a little alarmed.

"It is this. It concerns your little son."

Now she was alarmed! What about Marty?

"We are, as you know, childless, and we have a proposition to make to you that might benefit him."

"What is that?" Penny's heart began to hammer.

"We wish to make an offer of adoption."

She was conscious that they were looking at her keenly, especially her Mistress, whose face was flushed and whose breathing had become a little fast.

"Adoption?" she asked, her mouth dry. "You want to adopt Martin?"

"We would be able to give him everything he needs to set him up as a gentleman," Mr. Gordon continued. "Especially, a good education. He could go for the Law, or anything he chooses. He would have a secure future."

Penny was conscious that the colour had drained from her face, for it felt cold as ice.

"Adoption." she repeated, in a little panic.

"We do not need your answer now," Mrs. Gordon interposed, perhaps afraid that Penny would take her child and be gone before daybreak. "Think about it for a time. Take your time. We know how much you love him. We would have to find you another situation, many miles away, to make the separation complete, for we would expect him to think of us as his natural parents. It is a great deal to ask of you, I am sure, but we are just asking it, and you may think about it for as long as you wish, before he turns three, for that is when they begin to have memories."

The conversation ended there, she numbly promised to consider it.

Her heart said *No! No! No!* But her head pounded her, and disagreed. She went to bed straightaway, and lay there listening to the soft regular child-breaths of her baby as he slept, unaware that the future direction his life was to take, was being discussed.

How could she deny her son an education, the education she herself had craved? Education in a public school, years of education – reading, writing, mathematics, history, geography, the Classics, geometry, science, everything he would need for a good, good life! He could mix with sons of the peerage, he would visit their homes, meet their sisters – make a very fortunate marriage! Oh how could she deny him all of that which she had wanted so much for herself! Tears trickled down her face.

Before he turns three. Before he begins to have memories. Her darling son would grow up never knowing his own loving mother, not even remembering her! It was too much!

But as she thought and thought, another idea occurred to her. If she had to part with her son, should not the Eglintons have the chance to take him in and pay for his education? They could not hurt Martin now. Martin was dead. Perhaps even the old fellow was dead. There was nothing therefore to be lost by bringing her child to Manchester and introducing him to his relatives. And though sent to school by them, he could still call her Mamma, as she would find a small place for herself, a situation like this one, perhaps. The more she thought of it, the more determined she became.

CHAPTER SIXTY-EIGHT

Madame de Chantal was busy supervising an assistant pinning a length of Alençon lace to a puff sleeve when her new clients, Lady Kent and her daughter, arrived all the way from Manchester. She greeted them and bustled about making pleasantries in her usual way, before getting down to the business of measurements and choosing from her swatches of material. She was about to lead them into the back chamber when the street door opened, admitting a young lady of fashion, with a very elaborate hat and more than a little swagger.

"Good day, Madame de Chantal. Mr. Butler sent me."

Lady Kent and Miss Kent saw Madame's mood change instantly. She became red in the face and her manner took on that of a hissing cat.

"So he is back, is he? From his travels in Europe, at last? *Mademoiselle*, you can tell Mr. Butler that he is never to send anybody here again, after what happened to that unfortunate girl! You are, I suppose, his latest mistress! You should know that the last one threw herself under a carriage! The poor woman! So I said, never, never again will I take one *sou* from Mr. Butler! Begone!"

The woman turned bright red with indignation and she threw her chin in the air.

"You are quite wrong, Madame!" she said haughtily. "Mr. Butler told me the entire story himself! It was not Miss Fowler who died under the carriage, it was an intoxicated woman who had stolen her gown! He only found out after he had misidentified her! Miss Fowler is alive and well and lives under the patronage of a Mrs. Wells in Chiswick!"

This was a great shock to the Kents, for they knew immediately who Miss Fowler was. The story of the tragic woman who had ended her life under the carriage was well-known in Manchester. Penny was not dead then? But the Eglintons thought her so!

"I shall not patronise this establishment in any case," said the woman, who made as grand an exit as she had an entrance.

Madame apologised profusely to her clients for the disturbance, and they went to the back room in a daze.

"Mamma, what are we going to do about this?" Miss Kent asked upon vacating Maison de Chantal.

"Leave it alone, Alice. They were never married in the law, so she is no threat to you."

"But what if Martin finds out she is alive?"

"It does not make any difference. He chose you. You are to be Mrs. Eglinton."

"Mamma, she will come back to Manchester someday, and ruin our happiness! And was there not a child in the picture? She will bring back the child!"

Lady Kent appeared to think about this.

"The child was born outside wedlock; and will not impinge on the rights of any son you have."

"Mamma, we need to ensure that Miss Fowler never returns to Manchester."

"How are we to ensure that, Alice?"

"I do not know, Mamma. I thought her dead, and I know it's very wicked, but I wish she were! We can find her, and give her money to go to the continent."

"Nonsense! Who does she know on the continent? Persons of her rank don't go to Europe. But we will find this Mrs. Wells in Chiswick, and see what we will do after that."

"She was supposed to be dead!" muttered Alice, unhappily. "She was supposed to be dead!"

CHAPTER SIXTY-NINE

"**M**iss Fowler, there's nobody here with that name. Must be a wrong address, Madam." Said the butler.

"Oh that may be Mrs. Eglinton's maiden name." said Mrs. Gordon. "Take it to her."

Penny took the letter with the strange handwriting to a quiet corner, and opened and read it with great curiousity and a little trepidation.

Miss Fowler

I believe you call yourself Mrs. Eglinton. You are not entitled to use that name. Please desist. Also, you must never return to Manchester, because if you do, your life and that of your by-blow child will be in grave danger,

A Friend.

It was no friend who wrote that letter! Who could it be? It had the tone of Mr. Eglinton. But it was a female hand! She knew all the female hands of the Eglinton family! She was afraid, not so much for herself, as for little Marty. What kind of heart would threaten a child?

She could not return to Manchester! She did not know what to do. If Marty was to be educated, she had to give him up to the Gordons, and her heart ached.

CHAPTER SEVENTY

Martin had long thought of a trip to London, both for business and pleasure. He boarded a train south one day, arriving in London in the evening. His clumsy hand had necessitated his taking on a valet; his man, Woods, was a pleasant young chap who had never been to England's capital and was determined to enjoy himself there as much as time would allow. Claridges was a good beginning, he thought, even if Mr. Eglinton thought it was far too expensive. Woods knew why they were staying at Claridges. It was at the wish of Miss Kent, who he and the other servants privately dubbed *'the Empress'*, from what he had seen of her.

"Oh darling, here you are at last!" cooed Miss Kent later in the lobby. "I thought you'd come yesterday. I lay awake almost all of the night, wondering why you did not come! I have had a headache all day because of it. Haven't I, Mother?"

Lady Kent confirmed that she had suffered a headache.

"My dear, I did not tell you what day I would be here." Martin soothed her.

"Well now that you are here, do not leave me, not for a minute of the day!"

"Darling, I must see to my business." He said. "But, if you like, we can go tomorrow to see Kensington Gardens, and attend an Opera in the evening."

London must not be quite as bad as painted by Northerners, Woods thought, as he stole looks out the window on the fine street as he put away his master's clothes. He was very keen on seeing the City. He was enthused about the grand style of the London girls, but he thought the Mancunian girls had a great deal more natural beauty.

"There is no fear you shall fall in love then," said Martin with good humour, as Woods fixed his cravat on the first full day in Town.

"Oh no, sir, no fear at all! I want to see Brighton so much, the Pavilion especially, I was going to take a train down there, if that's all right with you, sir?"

"Perfectly all right, Woods. You may be free until evening."

"That's very good, sir!"

CHAPTER SEVENTY-ONE

Penny was deep in thought as she walked the beach, keeping a close eye on Marty, who was engaged in his favourite pastime, chasing seagulls with loud shouts, while flapping his arms. He fell every now and again, but picked himself up and cheerfully went on, finding another bird to chase as it hopped about looking for food on the shore.

It was a sunny day; the beach was packed with tourists. She loved Brighton; she loved the water; she loved living here. Her child was healthy in the invigorating sea air. Children ran about excitedly with buckets and spades while nannies and parents, seated on towels spread upon the sand, looked on. She heard the band play in the distance. Her thoughts returned to torment her.

Would she? Wouldn't she? The choice was agonising! Her heart was going to break.

Marty was chasing a large seagull, when the gull suddenly turned and making a loud noise and an energetic flapping of wings, began to half-fly, half-hop with an angry approach towards her son, who stopped abruptly in amazement. This sudden stop caused him to fall face-down into the sand. Penny, alarmed at the gull, screamed her son's name loudly. The bird was almost upon the toddler. A young man who was walking nearby darted forward, shooed off the bird, picked up her child and brought him to her.

"Oh thank you," she gasped, wiping off the sand from Marty's face, who did not at all seem perturbed by the incident. "He loves to run after the gulls, but I never saw one angry like that before! I was afeard 'e was going to peck his little head."

"No trouble, Missus. I say, you 'ave a bit of Lancashire in your accent, if you don't mind my saying so!"

"Oh I am a proud Mancunian!" she replied. "And from your accent, I think you are from thereabouts also?"

"I am. James Woods at your service, Missus." He bowed. "Have you lived 'ere long?"

"Two years here in Brighton, and before that I was in London for a time. I didn't like London. And you?"

"I'm just visiting. My master 'as business in London, he's putting up at Claridges in Grosvenor Square," he added, in a bragging way - "and I always 'ad a fancy to see the Brighton Pavilion. Well, I've just seen it, and it's not at all as grand as I thought it would be."

"I thought the same of the Pavilion, when I saw it. What kind of business is your master in? It must be a good one, that he can stay at Claridges!"

"Import business, Missus."

"Oh, tha's of interest to me! Might I enquire the name?"

"Eglinton Imports, Missus."

"Eglinton Imports! You don't say!"

"Why yes, Missus, do you know of them? I say, would you like to walk along a bit this way, might I be so bold as to ask?"

"Oh yes!"

"Egton, me Marty Egton!" said her son, pointing to himself.

"What's that, chappie?"

The boy chuckled, struggled to be put down, and he walked along beside the pair, holding Penny's hand.

"Eglintons. Of Clifton Walk?" Said Penny, uncertain as to how to proceed. The warning echoed. But she was very curious as to how all went on with the family. "I was in service there." she said.

"Were you indeed! That's a co-incidence! That 'ouse burned down." said Mr. Woods. "I'm valet to Mr. Eglinton."

"I found Mr. Eglinton very formidable." Penny said.

"Oh, he's easy to work for. And in very good humour, 'e's getting married again."

"Oh my goodness, did Mrs. Eglinton die?"

"She did. It was before I joined the family. A tragic accident, she fell under a carriage."

"I am very sorry to hear that, I was fond of her in a way."

"I 'eard," continued Mr. Woods. "though it might be a bit indelicate of me to say so, that she was in the family way when it 'appened."

"Mrs. Eglinton! In the family way!"

"Yes, that's what most people say. They find it 'ard to believe."

"She was too old – " Penny stopped abruptly. It was not decent to speak like this to a strange man. "And who is Mr. Eglinton about to marry?"

"A Miss Kent of Barton. Her father was knighted by Her Majesty." (another brag, Penny knew) "She and her mother, Lady Kent, are here too, buying of wedding clothes."

"I wish her very happy, I'm sure."

"You don't sound like you mean that, Missus, and to tell the truth, I don't like her, at least not for Mr. Eglinton. He's too good for 'er."

"Too good for her! He is a greedy man with a nasty tongue in 'is head! So selfish 'e is!"

"I never saw that, Missus, in 'im," said Mr. Woods, in an offended tone. "He's a decent gentleman. What I meant was, she can be bossy and mean to 'im, and jealous. My master is too decent a man to tell her off. Very brave too, not many went through what he went through, and be in continual good spirits. If you ask me, he's only marryin' her because she'll go all to pieces if he don't."

"I don't think we're speaking of the same Eglintons! What did 'e go through, as you put it? He was not fond of 'is wife! He led her a terrible life. I saw it!"

"I can't speak as to that. But there was a time, before I came, that 'e was unable to walk, but 'e's not a cripple now," Mr. Woods said. "My master walks very well, with a cane, but then many men use canes, that can walk perfectly. But then 'e got injured in the fire."

Penny had stopped dead. Mr. Woods, seeing her astonishment, went on.

"Mr. Eglinton saved 'is father, who could not make the stairs, on account of being laid up with a malady, and 'e it was carried 'im down, with the help of the footman. But 'e died later, two days later, and my master is left with a crippled 'and now."

Penny was dumbfounded. She tried to speak, but words practically failed her.

"Which Mr. Eglinton died?" she whispered.

"The old man!"

She did not need to ask, but she found herself saying the words.

"The Mr. Eglinton you serve. What – what is his Christian name?"

"Why, it's Martin. Mr. Martin Eglinton."

"Tha's me, Mamma!" Marty cried out. "Me Marty Egton!"

Mr. Woods looked down with indulgence at him, and then up at his mother, amused. She looked at Woods, a little fearfully, he thought, and swung her child into her arms once again.

"I must be off," she said. "It was nice talking to you, and thank you again."

"Why, is there summat the matter, Missus?"

"Martin did not die! Martin did not die!" she said aloud, and hurriedly, forgetting Mr. Woods completely in her turmoil, turning away, running up the sand toward the promenade, as fast as she could, leaving a very bewildered Mr. Woods looking after her.

CHAPTER SEVENTY-TWO

Penny was such a confusion of intense feeling that she did not know how to begin to organise her thoughts. They rushed at her one after another. She tried to reconstruct the conversation with Mr. Woods word for word as she hurried back to the house – but not wanting to go in as she would immediately have to take up her duties, and divert her mind from her present pressing occupation, she went past it and walked she knew not where, carrying her child, who had fallen asleep in her arms. She came to Victoria Park after a time, and sank down on the grass, exhausted, laying her child across her lap.

Martin was alive. Martin was recovered – recovered enough to have brought his father from a burning house! And Martin was getting married. No, no, how could he do that to her, when his father was dead, and presumably could not harm him now? It was obvious that the insanity diagnosis had been reversed, for he was now able to marry. *Why had he not found her?*

The carriage accident! Mrs. Eglinton – in the family way – died in a carriage accident!

It was her! It came upon her in a rush that Martin thought she was dead. That everybody in the Eglinton household thought she was dead.

Except one person – the one female who had written her the threatening note. It became very obvious to her now who might have been responsible for that.

But how to find Martin now? She had run from Mr. Woods, who she might have given a message for him! Why had she run?

She rose with the sleepy child in her arms, and brushed down her dress.

"Bless you child, you'll know your father yet! You shall be his son! You shall!"

The Eglinton Offices. Of course – that was where she would go tomorrow. Not to Claridges, certainly! It was in Mayfair, and too near Park Street.

Mrs. Gordon would not be too pleased that she would want more time off than the few hours in the afternoon that was hers, but it was imperative that she act as soon as she could. Mrs. Gordon, she could see, was getting uneasy at her hesitation to surrender Marty for adoption, and though she had been told to take her time, she sensed impatience.

CHAPTER SEVENTY-THREE

"Evening, Woods. Did you have a nice day at Brighton? Did you see the Pavilion? Is it worth a visit?"

"No sir, not at all." Woods took Mr. Eglinton's hat and cane, and said no more.

"Nothing to say at all about Brighton, then? Must have been a dull place."

Martin shot him a curious look. Woods was generally chatty, but he seemed quiet today, as if something unusual had occurred.

"What is it, Woods?" Martin sat down on a chair. He'd done a lot of walking and his legs ached.

Woods had been thinking all the way from Brighton. He thought he knew who the woman was.

"I met an interesting woman there, sir - "

"Oh now, Woods, you haven't gone and fallen in love already. I thought you preferred a Mancunian girl."

"It's not like that, sir, no, not at all. It is very curious, sir. A woman with a child about two years old. She was from Manchester and said she was in service in your house that burned down. She knew you, sir. She seemed to think that you were dead, sir, in the fire. When she realised it was your father that died, and that you were alive, she became upset, and said: *Martin did not die, Martin did not die*, an' ran off."

Martin froze, but his mind worked very quickly. A servant -? Only one had called him *Martin*. Only one.

"What was she like, Woods?"

"Not very tall, but bright eyes, blue. A keen look about her. Fair hair."

"Penny." He said immediately, very perplexed. "Is it Penny? Can she be alive? But why did I receive a letter saying that she was dead? Oh, Penny! Woods, did you see where she went?"

"I didn't see, sir, but I understood she lived local, and went there often, because she said her little boy always loved to run after the gulls. She called the little boy Martin, sir."

Woods turned away as his master's eyes filled with tears. It wouldn't do for him to notice it.

Though joyful that Penny was alive, Martin questioned whether she wished to see him. Why had Penny become upset and run off, he wondered to himself later. Was there another man in her life, and did she not want anything to do with him?

If so, he only had himself to blame. He had told her to make a life for herself.

He was engaged to be married, and it would be better to let this slide. Why hurt everybody, and himself also, by reopening a fresh wound? If he found Penny, and she rejected him – he did not think he could bear it. Why had she run off?

CHAPTER SEVENTY-FOUR

Penny agonised about her dress. Would she wear her best calico, which was green, or her older blue, blue being Martin's favourite colour? She remembered the time when her choices were between satin and silk! Would she take Marty? Yes, of course she would!

As she thought, Mrs. Gordon was not pleased. She felt that something was up and gave her permission very unwillingly, almost as if she knew that this would not turn out well for her.

Penny did not know where the Eglinton Import office was, so she had to make various enquiries, and found that it was most likely to be in the vicinity of the Docklands. She made her way there, very tired from walking and carrying Marty, who was becoming fretful. She began to worry as the afternoon wore on that the offices would close before she reached them. She stopped at a stall to buy a cold pie and they ate it between them. She bought Marty a cup of warm milk from a woman who sat on a stool, her milch-cow by her side. But she was nearing her destination. She could see India House, and Eglinton Imports, she had been told, was not far from there.

And there it was, a plain, ugly warehouse on the riverbank, with nothing to distinguish it from the other warehouses around it. She approached the door, her sleepy child in her arms, and experienced a sudden panic.

He would not expect to see her, for he thought her dead. Or did his man tell him of the encounter of yesterday? Suppose Martin realised it was her, but did not want to see her? What if he had learned about Mr. Butler, and was disgusted at her affair? Would he even believe that this was *his* child?

A few clerks came out and brushed past her as if she was not there. Of course, a poorly-dressed woman and her child, on the Docklands, was a common sight. She felt hardly different from the pathetic creatures she saw with barrows and carts. She looked down at her dress dusty from the streets, and knew that her exertions had done away with all trace of the cologne she had applied that morning, leaving the stale odour of sweat in its place. Poor little Marty smelt badly too; he was still in clouts and needed to be changed.

She could not allow Martin to see them like this. Poor, abject, beings! She had to refresh herself and her son, to present themselves! She became painfully aware that Miss Kent was most likely very elegant, scented of roses or violets, and her hands were lily-white and smooth. She probably carried a pretty parasol to protect her face from freckles.

She walked away. She had to think. She would not go back to Brighton tonight. She had money for a boarding house. She would go there and bathe Marty and freshen herself up, find a bite to eat, have a night's sleep, and tomorrow, she would go to Spitalfields to see Bernice O'Hara, get her advice, and borrow some fresh clothes.

Mrs. Gordon would be angry that she had not returned.

CHAPTER SEVENTY-FIVE

"**A**h is it yourself, alanna?" cried Bernice when she opened the door of the Shelter. "And this is your little laddie? Halloo little man!" she cooed, chucking him under the chin.

Penny's worries and anxieties fell away as Bernice wrapped her in a big hug and ushered her into the tiny parlour while she called for a pot of tea to be brought.

"How have you been all this time? You wrote, but I can't write well, so I didn't write back – what brings you here? Not trouble, I hope!"

Over tea, Penny related all that had happened in the last several weeks; the offer of adoption, and the encounter of the day before yesterday, which had led her to London. Bernice listened carefully.

"You were right to take your time and be prepared," she said. "I have a nice lacey shawl that I got for my niece's weddin' in June. And your bonnet – let's trim it with a bit o' new ribbon, will we? Not that he won't love you the way you are, dearie, but if you're feeling well about your appearance, that gives you faith in yourself, And never mind going down to the Docks again, you'll end up in the same state you were in yesterday. Go to the Hotel! I'll treat you to the cab fare!"

CHAPTER SEVENTY-SIX

"Whatʼs the matter, darling? You havenʼt spoken to me all day! Youʼre sulking! I wonʼt have you sulking, Martin."

"Iʼm not sulking, Alice. Iʼm thinking. Iʼm a quiet person. Sometimes, I do not talk a lot."

"As long as you are not thinking of *her*."

Martin rose and paced the floor of the sitting room that was a part of Lady Kentʼs suite of rooms. He felt a row brewing.

"Alice, we have to have a talk, you and I, about the future. No, donʼt cry. Be a rational human being, and talk to me."

But Alice was sobbing.

"You donʼt love me!"

Martin did not reply. He walked to the window and looked out rather absently, feeling defeated, and a little desperate. His attention was arrested by a young woman crossing the road, and his mind rushed back to when he used to watch for Penny out the window of his room. That step was Pennyʼs, firm and decisive, the woman had her air and demeanour, and with a great sudden leaping of his heart, he realised that it was – it was Penny! Instead of a hamper on her hip, she carried now a small child.

"Martin, you are so cruel to me! I told you before! Look at all I'm prepared to put up with, for you! Are you not listening, Martin? Where are you going?"

He was across the room, and left without a word, only pausing to take his cane. He banged the door behind him, while she screamed his name in growing hysteria.

CHAPTER SEVENTY-SEVEN

Martin descended the stairs rapidly. He reached the lobby in time to see a very snooty porter ask Penny what her business was, and looked at the toddler who held her hand tightly.

"Penny! Penny!"

"Martin! It is you! It is!"

Their eyes swam with tears of speechless joy, before he led her to a little alcove, hidden from public view, where they embraced tightly.

Penny took little Marty in her arms.

"Martin Eglinton, meet your son," she said.

"Me Marty Egton!"

"You're walking again," Penny said, her delight shining in her eyes. "I never knew you were so much taller than me, Martin Eglinton! I've a crick in my neck looking up at you!"

He laughed. He bent to whisper in her ear.

"And even better than that – I was declared of sound mind."

"You were always sound!" she hugged him suddenly, fiercely.

An angry female voice intruded upon their happiness.

"You there, tell me where Mr. Eglinton went, this minute!" The desk clerk knew of course, where Mr. Eglinton was, but was pretending he did not know.

Martin looked about, embarrassed, then loosed his embrace of Penny.

Somebody must have directed Miss Kent to the alcove, for she appeared there. She was just as Penny imagined – elegant, sweet-smelling, with a high hat.

"Martin, what is this? Who is she?" She pointed at Penny as if she were a prisoner in the Dock.

"Alice, this is my first – I mean, that is - " Martin floundered a little.

Penny was rummaging rather savagely in her reticule, and she drew out a letter.

"Did you write this?" she waved it to the woman, in an angry tone.

"How would I know, when I have not seen what is in it?" there was a sneering tone to her voice, but Penny detected a tremor of fear. She read it aloud.

Miss Fowler

I believe you call yourself Mrs. Eglinton. You are not entitled to use that name. Please desist. Also, you must never return to Manchester, because if you do, your life and that of your by-blow child will be in grave danger,

A Friend.

Penny gave the letter to Martin, who scanned it with astonishment.

"I most certainly did not write that. I have never seen you before in my life." Said Miss Kent.

"It is in your hand, Alice," Martin said slowly. "It is in your hand, this threat to the life of Penny and the child! How could you!"

"I didn't mean it. It was simply to frighten her away."

"You knew Penny was alive, and allowed me to go on believing she was dead?"

"I only found out the other day, from Madame de Chantal, tailoress to Mr. Butler's women, of which Miss Fowler appears to have been one, by the way."

Penny looked down and blushed. Martin stepped protectively toward her, while little Marty, seeing his mother upset, ran to the offender and smeared something on her dress.

She screamed.

"A worm! A dead worm! Oh you nasty little boy!" She made as if to strike him, but Penny intervened, pushing her away. She ran, screaming for the concierge.

CHAPTER SEVENTY-EIGHT

Mr. Eglinton was ejected from Claridges, an event he heartily welcomed.

"It was far too expensive," he said to Penny later, lounging on the grass at Primrose Hill, where they had come for the day. "I'm not wealthy, by the way. I am not the businessman my father was."

"What does it matter?" said Penny. "As long as you're happy. I can't tell you how I felt when I heard you were alive! It was a great moment!"

"But you ran away; Woods told me." He chewed a blade of grass.

"I remembered the threat." She looked fondly at Marty, playing on the grass.

"I don't know where he got the dead worm this morning," said Penny. "I can't take my eyes off him!"

"It was very noble of him to defend you. Will you marry me again, Penny?"

"Yes, I'll marry you again! I 'ope this will be the last time!"

"Aitches, Penny!"

They laughed.

"I have my eye on a house, not as big as Eglinton House, but big enough. We'll have shelves and shelves of books. I say, do you remember the day I showed you around the House, I had just hit you with a cricket ball and wanted to make it up to you. Then every Thursday, I used to watch you coming in with the hamper of washing, and I used to so look forward to seeing you walk up the driveway."

"How impertinent!"

"Do you mind, about Butler?" she asked, after a long moment. She hung her head as she put the question.

"Mother and I talked of it once, and we understood the desperate situation you were in. And we, the Eglintons, had created it."

Marty came up then, with his fist loosely closed around something.

"Papa back from 'Eaven. Present for Papa." He opened his fist and offered Martin a live beetle.

Papa took the beetle with great solemnity upon his forefinger, named him Bartlett, placed him carefully on a blade of grass and together they all watched him climb to the top and down the other side.

"We are going to be a very happy family," said Penny with contentment. "And I hope there will be brothers and sisters for Marty! Poor Mrs. Gordon," she said then, suddenly remembering. "I have to go to her, and explain. She was good to me."

Martin took her hand. "You have become – more kind." he said.

"I hope so, Martin. I was a girl from the slums, and I dreamed of being rich. When I became so, it went to my head. I lost it all, and suffered a great deal, and learned what was really important. Love and charity."

"I was very angry with my father." Martin admitted. "I lay abed all that time, unable to walk, and spent a lot of time asking God: '*Why*?' When I saw Father on his deathbed, burning up in agony, and begging my forgiveness, I wanted more than anything to – do anything I could for him. If I hadn't forgiven him, I would have carried that weight around, and it would have been heavier than anything I endured in Peru and after."

"Penny, shall we marry the day after tomorrow, and set off for Manchester?"

"Go to Manchy, Mamma!"

"I think it's been decided upon." Penny laughed.

THANK YOU FOR CHOOSING A PUREREAD BOOK!

We hope you enjoyed the story, and as a way to thank you for choosing PureRead we'd like to send you this free book, and other fun reader rewards…

Click here for your free copy of Whitechapel Waif
PureRead.com/victorian

Thanks again for reading.
See you soon!

LOVE VICTORIAN ROMANCE?

If you enjoyed this story why not continue straight away with other books in our PureRead Victorian Romance library?

Read them all...

Victorian Slum Girl's Dream

Poor Girl's Hope

The Lost Orphan of Cheapside

Born a Workhouse Baby

The Lowly Maid's Triumph

Poor Girl's Hope

The Victorian Millhouse Sisters

Dora's Workhouse Child

Saltwick River Orphan

Workhouse Girl and The Veiled Lady

OUR GIFT TO YOU

AS A WAY TO SAY THANK YOU WE WOULD
LOVE TO SEND YOU THIS BEAUTIFUL
STORY FREE OF CHARGE.

Click here for your free copy of Whitechapel Waif

PureRead.com/victorian

At PureRead we publish books you can trust. Great tales without
smut or swearing, but with all of the mystery and romance you
expect from a great story.

Be the first to know when we release new books, take part in our
fun competitions, and get surprise free books in your inbox by
signing up to our free VIP Reader list.

As a thank you you'll receive a copy of Whitechapel Waif straight
away in you inbox.

Click here for your free copy of Whitechapel Waif

PureRead.com/victorian

Printed in Great Britain
by Amazon

45078943R00148